A Violent Hope

Ericka Clay

Published by Believable Books, 2020.

A VIOLENT HOPE

First edition. October 6, 2020.

ISBN: 979-8681470717

Written by Ericka Clay.

To Jesus. For saving my life.

"The Lord is near to the brokenhearted and saves the crushed in spirit." Psalm 34:18

People are beautifully curious.

    They cut themselves. They want healed.

They burn themselves. They want healed.

They burn others. They want justification.

But beyond all that, they just want love.

They live in their homes where their noise buzzes, a constant in their heads. And there's never enough quiet to hear what I'm saying inside of their hearts.

There are always a few, though. A broken few who seek the slightest shadow of my face. And I reveal it as I look down, and they look up from the darkest parts of themselves. They quietly search me with their eyes. They dare to hope, a violent kind of endeavor.

And when I reach my hand down, when they take it, everything's unlocked, inside out.

The truth breaks free.

And so do they.

Then

Chapter One

Mack is six-years-old, and man, is he a beautiful boy. He has this shy little smile and such clear blue eyes. They've cut his hair into a bowl cut that sits above his eyebrows, and his shirt is striped and dirty with jelly stains. They don't dress him or clean his clothes like they should.

They don't do a lot of things they should, really.

But I love them, too, and I guess that's always the hardest part for a heart to understand.

His best friend is Roy McGruffin, a nearly threadbare police officer that moonlights as a stuffed dog toy. Mack got him when he was three from a cop on a street corner handing out recruiting fliers to the adults and toys to the kids. The police officer told Mack the dog's name was Roy McGruffin so Mack committed it to memory even though his tongue couldn't quite handle the "gr" sound yet. Sometimes Mack thinks of the police officer and assumes he's still standing on that corner. His name is Kevin, but he's no longer there. In fact, he died last year breaking up a domestic dispute. Bullet straight through his heart. His death was like looking through a kaleidoscope, everything touching and turning. There was the grief that almost swallowed his parents and ex-wife whole.

But then there was this new shock of color and shape in the lens. Everyone began to trust each other with their hearts.

Mack takes Roy everywhere which is why a lot of his fur has rubbed away, and he has a grubby feel to him. But these are things people only notice if they're paying attention.

"Mack, you remember now, right? I'll leave the key under the mat. You get off the bus, you go down the sidewalk, up the stairs, and open the front door. Wait here. Make a snack. No oven, no microwave. Uncle Dennis will come by when he gets off work so just wait for him. TV's okay but just cartoons. You got it?" Rochelle Reynolds is exasperated by the end of this little spiel like she can already see in her mind's eye Mack walking down the wrong sidewalk or entering the wrong duplex. Rochelle is very OCD and even now presses a Virginia Slim against her lips in hopes of curbing the way her brain thinks. I didn't create it to be such a burden. In fact, there are so many beautiful things about Rochelle's brain but the downfall is when she lets the voices get a little too loud. She gets paranoid. Her heart closes its eyes and pretends I don't exist. But deep down Rochelle knows that's a lie.

"'Member," Mack says because he's about to get on the school bus and is too distracted by the fact that he'll be separated from Roy McGruffin for several hours. Rochelle outlined what school would be like, and Mack has been infinitely perturbed about it. He lets his thoughts be a distraction now, and Rochelle sighs hard through her nostrils.

"Pray you make it through the day," she mutters and grabs her purse. She presses her lips against his forehead, swipes at the permanent jelly stains, and takes his hand. She walks him to the bus stop which is across the street from their duplex. After another wet kiss against hair and skin, he watches his mother dash across the road in her "good" clothes. Rochelle just landed a temp job as a secretary for a pretty prominent Texarkana lawyer, and word on the street (or in the break room) is that the former secretary won't be coming back. Rochelle hopes this is her big break.

Mack, however, feels empty, like he could fly away even though his backpack and his Wild Wild West lunch box weigh down his tiny body.

The bus comes. He goes to school, and it's not that bad.

But then he comes home.

He makes the snack—crackers and cheese whiz—and pours orange juice into a cup but mostly on the floor. He watches *The Deputy Dawg Show*. He practices forgetting until Dennis walks through the front door.

Dennis. His heart has always been the feel and weight of rock. Even as a child, he'd pluck the wings off a fly and study its pain before slowly working it into the sidewalk with his thumb. I've studied Dennis from all angles: his choices, his parents who always turned a blind eye. They took Dennis to church, but they never taught Dennis about me. I was waiting so long for Dennis, but that door was slammed hard in my face.

At some point, your knuckles get sore from knocking.

There's always a nefarious tether between Dennis and Mack. It's all Dennis, all in his eyes and the way he leers at my beautiful boy and wants to make him his. The dark is deep inside him. A well with no water at the bottom.

Mack turns off the TV when Dennis comes in wearing his janitor's uniform. Mack wants to continue watching, pretending he's so enthralled with the show that nothing can tear him away and paste him back into reality.

Dennis nods, gives him the signal. And he takes my beautiful boy to his bedroom with the chair and the rope.

Chapter Two

Mack is eleven-years-old, and man, does he wear his heart in his eyes. I'm wary of that look, part spark, part deep disconnection. He's rough along all of his edges and won't open the door even though I've used several modes of knocking. Belinda, his fifth grade teacher who wears a cross across her throat, is extra gentle with him. She speaks softly when she points out his math mistakes, and when he asks her why she wears it, she puts her fingers against the cross and explains that she's a Christian. She's not like the others, the ones who say it but like to stroke the dark with their hands. Belinda is all light, and Mack can sense it in her face.

Another time, Mack tries out for the fifth grade basketball team, and Jeremy Liotta is the coach. Mack is absolutely terrible at basketball but doesn't seem to truly understand this. Jeremy spies the kid with the dirty fingernails and hair in his eyes. He sees his younger self in Mack's beat up expression because Jeremy was left for dead when he was three. His parents were barely survivors of the Depression, and when they moved states, they left Jeremy behind in their dismal rental.

Mack didn't make the team, but Jeremy did try to reach out to Rochelle to see if he could take him to lunch some time. Dennis answered the door.

"No, sir. The kid's just fine. I'll be sure to spend more time with him," Dennis said as he roughly closed the door in Jeremy's face.

One night, Rochelle is asked out for drinks after work. The whole team's going, even Glenn Augustus, lead DA at Augustus, Norton, and Davies. He asks Rochelle personally, and she just can't say no even though it's Friday game night with Mack and Dennis.

"You understand right?" She's flipping the curlers out of her hair, brushing it hard against her head. She slips on her heels and grabs her bag, her lips landing on their usual target on Mack's forehead. Her scent is too frank, like syrup.

"Sure," Mack says, single syllables being his favorite kind of response these days.

"We'll be just fine," Dennis says, putting his arm around Mack. Mack tells his brain to relax his face. When Rochelle leaves, he shoulders Dennis off him.

"Big man? That the game we're playing tonight?" Dennis turns off the TV, and the room goes silent. He's still between Mack and the front door Rochelle's just closed. Dennis believes no one is watching, and Mack is asking where I've run to. *Here, Mack. Right here,* I say. He presses his fist against his breastbone and takes a deep breath.

"No," Mack says. Dennis nods and bumps him as he heads to the kitchen.

"It's a macaroni kind of night," he sings out, head stuffed in a cabinet.

"It always is," Mack says.

• • • •

ROY MCGRUFFIN SITS high on a wooden shelf above Mack's window. His room faces out to the street. Mack plants his face against it, watches kids from his class, from his school playing out in the middle of it. He doesn't bother with them because they don't understand him. But there is one kid who got kicked out of ninth grade and goes to the school across town now. His name is Leonard, and Leonard is so alone on the inside that he laughs extra loud and makes people think he's funny. Mack doesn't see the appeal, but he does see the appeal in what Leonard brings him.

Leonard is on the sidewalk and looks like a sharp shard of glass in the sea of children. Everyone instinctually gives him breathing room.

Mack nods at him which is Leonard's signal to come in. They're the same size, Leonard and Mack, even though Leonard is three years older. His mother drank during the pregnancy and barely ate. Her head is a demonic cloud of mis-thoughts so that when she looks in the mirror, all she can see is her own ugliness. When she looks at Leonard, she doesn't see much better.

"Creeper here?" Leonard asks, nodding at Dennis's bedroom.

"Nah." Mack shuts the black curtains he asked Rochelle to buy to help him sleep. His room is shaded in dark except for a slit of light that slices the wood floor. Leonard takes the bean bag chair in the corner. He takes out his tin with the papers and lighter and a baggie full of weed out of his jeans pocket. He rolls a joint and lights it.

"Your turn," he barely eeks out as he passes it to Mack. He thinks he must seem like a god in Mack's eyes, but Mack only feels deeply sorry for him.

When Mack breathes in the dirty air, his muscles relax. His brain is insignificant, and he can't feel his heartbeat. He's belly down on his bed, and he tries to ignore Roy McGruffin glaring down at him.

They smoke for a little while longer, listening to Free Bird on his Fisher Price record player. He should be embarrassed about that, about Roy who hovers above them, but Mack doesn't feel anything. It's why he lets Leonard dance with him.

They dance slow, and he knows Leonard will try to kiss him. He sees the scene in his head because they've played it over and over every Saturday evening, when dusk is still outside his curtain and his uncle's at work, his mother's at Glenn's place, spending the night. He should say no. He should say and do a lot of things.

But Mack is only human. Something he tries so hard to forget.

Chapter Three

Mack is sixteen-years-old, and man, does he have a mouth on him. He talks like a sailor and anger is woven through every inch of his clothes. He wears all black and his favorite bands are Slayer and Bathory. His brain breaks into puzzle pieces when he listens to it, and when he comes to, it's like a deaf and dumb surgeon tries to put him back together again.

He's sentenced Roy McGruffin to the back of his closet. Leonard's been sentenced to FCI Texarkana, the city's finest correctional facility, which suits Mack just fine.

His body is bigger, more filled out now. Even Dennis is scared to look him in the eye.

Rochelle is working through her own journey. She's absorbed *You Can Heal Your Life* like a salve on the skin. She's taken her existence in her own hands and is roughly repurposing it. She's just forgotten to assess the deep gash working between her feet and Mack's.

"I am beat," she says. She smells like sweat and looks ridiculous in a neon pink headband and wrist warmers. She's all spandex and endorphins, and Mack can barely look at her. Her room is sparse now, just a few outfits and toiletries to remind Mack he had a mother once. She lives mostly at Glenn's and has been dragging her feet the past five years, working up the courage to officially move in and bring her son with her. But her son won't speak to her.

He grabs his bag and doesn't even grunt a reply. He's the star of the wrestling team even though he's only a junior, but Mack looks like he'd rather put a curse on the team than be a part of it. He tries not to turn into a self-help nitwit himself and diagnose his feelings of abandonment and the sick feeling of not being enough anymore, not even for Dennis.

Before he leaves the front stoop of the duplex, he punches his fist into the wall next to the door. He lives on that pain and breathes through it as he walks to Saturday morning wrestling practice. He doesn't hang out with the team like he should, other than the pizza parties and canned food drives they put on to raise money. They all seem...content. Like they've each found the outline of themselves and have snugly shouldered their way into them.

Mack feels like he's free floating. And nobody is even attempting to swipe him back down to the ground anymore.

"What's this?" Coach Markle says as Mack walks into the locker room. He's there early before anyone else is so he can change in private. He tries not to diagnose that either.

"Oh, I don't know. Just got a little upset," he says, trying to shrug off the gash in his knuckles. Coach Markle nods. Markle's always been like so many people I watch and love. There is an edge of goodness in him, one I want so desperately to grow. And here's a moment I could watch the roots take hold into the soil, but he rips up the plant just like every other time.

"Good. Use that anger," he says, and he doesn't realize it's like a nail in the coffin.

Chapter Four

Mack is twenty-one-years-old, and man, is he over it. His anger is subdued like a feral kitten, small but still in full force. He keeps it locked down, and whenever he goes to look for me, he finds it instead. Sometimes he pets it. Sometimes he leaves it alone.

He graduated high school with a wrestling scholarship to Texas A&M-Texarkana, but he decided not to go. He thought about it for a while, but the kitten kept nipping at him, and he thought to himself: *Why do I think I can do any better?*

It was an expected reaction, but his mother was so disappointed. Glenn Augustus was disappointed, too, because it meant a potential freeloader looking for a handout. Glenn is a staunch Republican and is still sore from Clinton winning the presidency. He detests the tactless phrase "trickle-down economics," but he fully embodies the theory, splattering the world with his financial investments. He has a sixth sense when it comes to his money, and I admire his keen intellect and the lack of fear in his heart. But not much else.

"You can do better, Mack. We can help. Glenn wants to help." Glenn is in the threshold of Mack's apartment, the sun edging his Lacoste polo, almost giving him the impression of an angelic being. But Mack doesn't look at him. He hardly looks at this mother because the kitten is shrieking fiercely in his chest.

"I'm sure he does." Mack is eating Fruit Loops at the breakfast bar at his apartment like a child. He's graduated from trade school and has worked for the past year at Estes Auto Repair where Jaime Estes treats him like family. He respects Jaime, a feeling he once carried around for the father he's never met until Rochelle told him in a drunken stupor once how his father was a rapist who took his own life.

It was like digging up a treasure chest only to find it empty.

"Look, we care about you. And I know you are capable of so much more. You did so well in high school. That was all you, I know that.

You kept your grades up and worked so hard on the wrestling team. Don't give up on yourself. Let Glenn pay for your schooling. You can stay with us–or Dennis? Dennis would love for you to stay with him." Mack snorts on a Fruit Loop and tries to keep it from going down the wrong pipe. He takes a big swig of his chocolate milk trying to forget but instantly remembering Dennis's face the day he left the duplex for good. His mother was working, so Mack loaded his stuff up in Coach Markle's borrowed pick up himself. Dennis kept shadowing the threshold of his room like Glenn does now.

"All grown up," Dennis said. The insanity had already eaten a large chunk of his brain, and his heart was so small at this point, it could barely be felt. His mind's eye was a dismal fabrication of what uncles typically do with nephews. There were trips to the park and walks with invisible dogs. And a blatantly senseless feeling of respect between the two of them. When Mack looked at him in the doorway, he couldn't see anything but an outline framed in black.

"That's the word on the street," Mack said. He wasn't scared or even threatened. He could have killed Dennis if he wanted to. He just didn't feel like it. He was thinking about the money he'd be making, his brand new apartment. About going to some bar and getting toasted and hopefully meeting a girl. He thought these were the necessary steps to a better life, like he could dig up the old one and firmly replace it. But he didn't understand that the past is stamped permanently. That it's tattooed on every inch of his insides unless he lets me in to wash it clean.

"Dennis?" he asked. He retrieved Roy McGruffin from a dirty corner of his closet to put him in a box.

"What, buddy?" Dennis asked, hopelessly hopeful.

"Nothing." Mack said because that's exactly the way he felt.

"You okay?" Rochelle asks now, tentatively patting him on the back. It's a breach of his personal bubble, and it reminds him of wrestling, of feeling somebody tangled all up with you and how you never feel alone in a moment like that.

"Yes," Mack says firmly, feeling the kitten growl a little bit in his chest. "I'm perfectly fine."

• • • •

THERE'S A WOMAN AT the bar he's never seen before. And before the night is over, she's in his bed. He's too drunk to say anything, but she feels like a dream, like the only thing that can save his soul.

I've planted her hard in his life. It's his last and final hope.

He's so drunk and sweating, he can't make heads or tails of anything except the white sheets he's swimming in. Natalie helped him back to his apartment because she already knows this is the man she's going to marry. But she would have done it anyway knowing her.

She's stripped him down to his underwear after he vomited on his shirt. I helped her pick up his large body so she could move him from the toilet to the bed. She wipes the stink and sweat off of him and doesn't even mind when he tries to kiss her with his foul mouth.

"Just rest," she says and holds his hand. He begins to cry.

"What is it?" she asks.

And that is the key that unlocks him. He tells her about Dennis, and Leonard, and Roy McGruffin. He tells her his stupid mistake of turning down his scholarship and what Rochelle and Glenn think of him. Natalie's heart is good soil. It's abundant and deep, and she plants every word so she can tend to each individually.

"I'm sorry," is all he can keep saying as she lightly kisses his hairline that still smells like Jager Bombs.

"Don't be," she says and holds him in her arms. She's not afraid of his brokenness or threatened by his past. She's one of the good ones.

So for one night, Mack forgets about the darkened room, the ropes. He forgets about being exposed and touched and tormented.

About being a child.

Chapter Five

M ack is twenty-six-years-old, and man, is he tired.

Mack looks at his hands and tries not to look at his wrists. But that's an impossible feat, so instead of looking at the lines crawling over his palms, he rolls his forearms back and forth to see the white, faded lines that fit like shirt cuffs.

Mack sits in their living room, checking on those wrists, wondering if the past can ever be unbraided from a person's soul and maybe what that would feel like. He keeps rotating, feeling all the gut punches, the stink of hot breath on a person's neck, barely noticing when his daughter, Wren, puts her tiny hands on his. She covers the heart tattoo he got a few years ago, the night he moved out of the duplex. He forces himself to look up and hugs her tight because he's her whole world, and he doesn't have the heart to tell her he's only a man.

They spend the day together and go home eventually after ice cream and shopping around for car parts. Mack still works for Jaime Estes and Jaime pays him a little extra on the weekends to look for things they might need at the shop. Wren loves Saturdays because of Mack and the ice cream but also because she gets to feel and hold things she doesn't usually get to. She's very tactile and learns life through her hands, a lot like her father.

They're home now, so Mack showers and changes and rubs his fingers over Wren's hair. He gives Natalie a kiss, and Natalie feels a little numb to it which she'll always regret later on.

His hands are behind his back, and he has Wren's attention. She tries to swipe at them to see what he's hiding, but he keeps the game going a little longer and relishes the moment. He looks down at her. At the soft curls of her four-year-old head that are straightening. At the blonde in her hair that is darkening. He takes a permanent picture in his brain and then lets his arms go free.

"A puppy." Wren says, and he smiles. No, not a puppy. More like a stuffed dog that's seen too much.

"His name is Roy McGruffin, but you can call him whatever you want."

"I like Roy. Roy, let's go." She whispers and hugs on Mack's leg before dragging the dog to her room. Natalie looks at the man she always knew she would marry and smiles, but the sadness clings to it.

"I love you," he says and presses his lips into her hairline. *I know*, she thinks but doesn't say, just lets herself be held. She doesn't even watch him leave as he heads out the door to the bar.

Outside, he smells the air as if he's assessing his situation, this type of life that's wrenched him out of the car and left him on the side of the road. And you don't know how many times I've laid my hand on his shoulder and whispered in his ear, but the man gives into the dark little kitten inside his chest. Rochelle called this morning. Dennis is dying and wouldn't it be nice if Mack went over and spent some time with him?

So Mack drives, rubbing his fist into his temple and then smacking his temple too hard with it. "Why?" he forms beneath his breath, and his tires take him somewhere he doesn't want to go.

Dennis still lives in the duplex. Rochelle lives on the other side of town now with Glenn Augustus where she gets older and asks me for forgiveness. And I give it over and over again because I know the love inside her. And I know she's failed, but the thing is, at least she can admit it.

Mack looks up and feels the duplex before he sees it. He's spent all these years living in the same town yet living a world apart. There have been shadows of Dennis–half an ear turning down a grocery aisle, a stray arm leaving the dentist–but Mack's never had to fully look him in the face since the day Rochelle married Glenn Augustus.

He rings the doorbell. His hands are sweaty and his body sober. He should have hit the whiskey, he thinks, but there's none in the house. One of Natalie's rules.

He hears shuffling. Every nerve goes blank.

"Hullo." Dennis's mouth is shoved in the crack between door and frame. There's flight but no fight in Mack. His legs are too dull to run so Mack says "hello" back.

"Mack, oh my word. Mack," Dennis says and shoves open the door. The smell is so rancid, Mack is able to taste it. I can see them playing in the corner–the demons–even though Mack can't. They balk and whine. They struggle against each other like they're trapped.

They feel me watching them.

"Boy, come in. Come in and see Uncle Dennis." Mack walks in and shuffles over loose pieces of floor. He realizes they're magazine pages. His mother hasn't been here because Dennis won't let her. He told her she made her choice years ago, running off with that pretty boy, Glenn Augustus. And Rochelle doesn't challenge him on it because she's on the cusp of understanding what her brother really is.

Dennis takes Mack past the bedrooms, his old bedroom, and Mack tries not to form thoughts in his head. They move past the living room to the back of the duplex where the kitchen is.

"Sit. There's more than enough." Dennis is indicating that the macaroni and cheese he's made in an unwashed pot is more than enough for them to share. Eating, breaking bread. There's a moment where I'm on his heart, and something from a long time ago is nailed to the cortex of Mack's brain. Church.

They had gone twice when Rochelle momentarily dated the man who changed the oil in her Le Sabre. It was a circus. All these beautiful children running and whooping about in a large gymnasium at Trinity Grace Presbyterian. They were nice enough, Mack guessed. But what really hit him was when they were squeezed into a back hallway, and into tiny crackerjack box classrooms that smelled of kid sweat and candy. And there was a woman with a Bible who read from Mark. The bread, the body. The cup, the blood. Take and eat. Believe.

In what? Mack asks me and closes his arms across his chest.

"I'm okay," he says to Dennis. A tiny worm of nausea is growing fatter in his stomach. He takes control and beats it down until it's barely wiggling. His forehead is damp.

"Mack. Mack buddy, you feeling okay?" Dennis comes towards him. His dirty nails are clawing at the air in front of Mack and the movement reveals yellowish stains where wife beater meets armpit. Mack's insides struggle like the demons watching us. His movements trigger his memory, and the parched word is offered into the air: "Why?"

"Why? Why what?" Dennis is genuinely confused. He's caught up in it, the demonic energy that vibrates through his veins. Accusations aren't reality. Reality isn't reality. He constructs the truth with a decaying mind.

"You know."

"No, Mack. I don't. You feeling okay? You want some water?" Dennis points at a dirty cup with water, tinged gray. He takes it for himself, gulps it down then offers it to Mack. The worm grows fierce in Mack's belly, and he can no longer keep it still. He's going to vomit, and for a moment, the demons forget themselves and settle with a hopeless sort of hope. But then I shine and burn until I can hear them sizzle.

"Bathroom," Mack says and doesn't wait for direction. The duplex is inside of him, and he closes his eyes as he passes Dennis's bedroom. The smell, the feel of the grimy counters doesn't help. There's feces clinging to the upper lip of the toilet, and Mack has the urge to rip it from the floor, but he's too busy releasing into the bowl.

He weakens, and his back is sliding down the bathroom wall. The feel of the wooden chair against his naked thighs. The rope. His wrists sting, and his tears sear his face. It's the wrong thing to do to look in the mirror.

He rips open the door and finds Dennis, struggles him against the kitchen wall.

"Why! I asked you why!" he screams. Dennis looks up, the delusion painted thick on his face. "Why did you hurt me?" Mack barely registers that he's touching Dennis but still, he registers it. The man's skin is warm and thin and something like empathy confuses Mack's brain. Mack gets it. He's nothing like Dennis. He knows the weight and feel of compassion, but suddenly, he takes his hands and strangles it.

Dennis's warm, thin skin turns a shade of palish blue. Mack thinks right now that he's getting even. Settling that score. But death has nothing to do with winning.

Mack squeezes so hard until Dennis is lost to me forever. Mack slides down so that Dennis is a mess of limbs in Mack's lap, and for an instant, compassion revives itself. He's crying over his uncle, making words out of the jumbled letters in his head. He sounds like a donkey shot in the gut. But in a moment, just as quick as the last one, he's pushing Dennis off his lap and wiping his hands on his jeans. He leaves, the real score rearing its ugly head.

Later at the bar, there's a woman who tugs on his arm, and usually, Mack would shove her off, but he's too sad and drunk to do something like that. So instead, he dances with her, and they whirl so hard on the floor, the threat of vomiting overtakes him again. She leads him to a back closet near the bathrooms where it's dark, and her fingers feel like claws. Finally, he comes to a bit and wrestles her off. He stumbles back near the bar, grabs his coat. His buddy Leon who he works with at the shop waves at him, but Mack waves him off and heads to the door.

Mack doesn't take his truck home. He tries to get the key into the door, but his brain and hand won't work. So he walks.

The walk is cold but a good cold that smacks his face and works his legs. He doesn't like thinking of Dennis; who would, really? Dennis I loved, but Dennis most certainly did not love me back.

Mack thinks of the room, and the ropes, and the pain, and all the things I wish I could wash clean if only he'd let me. But he keeps walking on through his past until he gets home, and he finds the tree. It's the magnolia in their yard that Wren runs around until her little legs give out. He heads on to the shed and finds the coiled rope. It takes him an embarrassingly long amount of time to struggle it out onto the ground. Next, he finds the step stool because he can't trust his legs to climb.

Inside, Wren wakes up too early. It's still black around the edges of her blinds. The house is silent except for Natalie's TV. Wren chews on the knot in her throat because Natalie is the only one in bed. She stands on tiptoes at her parents' bedroom door–Roy McGruffin a permanent staple in her hand–and watches Natalie's eyes blankly scan the woman selling snow globes. Her fingers worry a scabby line into her lips. Wren and Roy tiptoe quietly again out into the hall.

Mack has knotted the noose, thrown the rope over the limb after four practice tries. He's stumbled and straightened, taking shaky step after shaky step. He's on the top step now where memory fights him. He battles with a broken tooth he received when he was Wren's age, wiping out on the wooden living room floor in his socks. He's eight, and his mother has beaten him at Yahtzee, and she's kissing him because he's crying but not because he's lost. He's fourteen, and Leonard is still in his bedroom, and his heart is still broken. He's sixteen and angry and keys a car for the sheer pleasure of it. He's twenty-two and marrying Natalie in a tiny gazebo, and never has he looked at anyone who deserves so much better. He's twenty-three, and his daughter Wren is in his hands. He's twenty-six, and his uncle is dead from the force of the same ones.

Memory loses, and he jumps. The rope tightens. Fear tightens. Everything touches and turns, and he sees their home for the first time swiveling before him. It starts to color and shape, and he can feel his daughter and wife inside. Love breaks open his heart, my beautiful boy, and for the first time, he understands. He confesses. He repents. He sees me and calls me inside. I take his hands, and then we go together to the room I've already prepared for him.

Wren softly unlocks the front door and goes to find her tree because she needs to touch it. But when she steps outside, there's an oversized fruit dangling from it. She squeezes closer to the fruit, squeezes Roy closer to her chest. Her hand goes skyward as if to pluck it down, but the fruit circles around out of her grasp. Once its boots point at her head, she knows what she's looking at.

Her father. My beautiful, Mack.

Wren has hardly ingested the way it tastes, seeing her father dancing above her, when Natalie opens the door and comes to her knees on the porch. She's run outside because Wren is screaming, but Wren can't feel the wind in her throat, or the vibration in her vocal chords, or even Roy in her hand.

She can only feel the empty space where her heart once was.

Chapter Six

Lying breast and belly against the porch, Natalie freezes time, and I let her. Her daughter is still screaming, and her husband dangles from a tree. But in Natalie's mind, it's five years ago, and she's living it with a hunger in her heart.

At the time, she didn't even want to live it at all.

• • • •

MACK IS HUNG OVER AND smells like death. She's spent the night hearing his sins and the sins that have been trespassed against him. Natalie sniffs her skin and smells the Jager and his sweat, but what's worse is the way her insides feel but mostly her mind. Its door is open and all has been plundered.

Natalie spills inside out as she finds his bathroom and closes the door. She takes a shower, dries off with a damp towel and puts her bar clothes on again. Her heart is still broken from her ex who left her two years ago for his dental hygienist. He went to Texas A&M-Texarkana. Business major. His family had more money than they knew what to do with but decidedly never spent any of it on his manners. He didn't even blink when he left her. Todd Hiney. Natalie Hiney. Maybe he did her a favor, she thinks.

So Mack was supposed to be a one night fling. A band-aid on a stitch-worthy flesh wound. She's never done something like this before and was almost relieved when Mack became stumble-drunk in an instant and started to relive his nightmare with her in his bed. She doesn't want sex. She wants fulfillment. So she figures she'll marry Mack. Better a broken man than self-possessed one.

She makes sure to put a glass of water on the nightstand and a bottle of Advil. She has her shoes in her hand and her purse clamped under her armpit, but as she turns, Mack grabs her hand. Her body moves quietly enough but her soul stirs him awake.

"Leaving." Mack declares it because the question would hurt his head too much.

"For now," she says, blessing his temple with a kiss because Natalie's one of the good ones.

She just doesn't know it yet.

• • • •

SHE MEETS HIS MOTHER and Glenn Augustus and nothing goes according to plan. They eat at Red Lobster and Natalie orders a hamburger off the kids menu since she's allergic to shellfish. Glenn Augustus looks appalled, and Mack smoothes over the situation by blurting out that he and Natalie are getting married even though he hasn't even asked her yet. She's not angry he does it like this. She's too wrapped up in the surprise and thrill of it and ignores the sharp edge of loving a man you know everything about and nothing at all.

• • • •

SHE ITCHES AND SWEATS in the Texarkana sun. Natalie wears the same dress Rochelle wore two years ago at her and Glenn's small wedding ceremony in Glenn's backyard. At that affair, Mack had gotten noticeably drunk and was ushered out by a very forlorn looking Dennis.

"Get off me!" Mack had growled and set off to walk home even though Dennis was opening the front door of Rochelle's barely mobile Le Sabre.

"You think it'll last?" Dennis asked, looking up at Glenn's enormous house. The fear was already playing chess with his head and heart, but Mack was too drunk to notice and too invested to care.

"What ever does?" Mack laughed at his own joke and that's the sound Dennis would replay for the longest time.

Mack's mother gave Natalie the dress like she was giving away her own life. Natalie could see the "I'm sorry" in Rochelle's eyes as easily as the tight stitching in the polyester/cotton blend. It makes her look like an office secretary but Mack thinks he sees an angel walking down the aisle runner. He's flanked by his boss, Jaime, and work friend, Leon. Dennis shifts around somewhere near the back of the standing crowd, and Natalie tries not to look at one of her husband's demons. At Natalie's side of the gazebo stands her sister, Rebecca, and cousin, Polly—two women who think this whole ordeal is a big mistake. The looks on their faces keep Natalie propelling forward down the makeshift aisle at Bringle Lake Park. The air smells like water and the future is intangible. But Natalie has created something like two rocks in her stomach. Something that sparks hope when she rubs them together.

Things will get better. They must.

• • • •

A YEAR IN CAN BE MEASURED in empty cans of beer and bottles of whiskey hidden around the house. Except that they're not hidden because Natalie is great at finding things, and Mack wouldn't know how to hide his own displeasure. She lets it slide at first, her sister and cousin's faces giving her a strange sense of determination. But after the second time he sleeps in and forgets to go to work, she says, "No more." They need to save up for a house. They need to have a baby. They need to get out of the apartment. Because those are the things that will change their lives for the better.

Natalie plays with the rocks and watches the light flicker.

She works, too. Natalie isn't lazy and has been working what feels like all her life. She didn't have the luxury of college, Rebecca still a teen and at home while their father broke his back at the lumber company. Their mother had died giving birth to Rebecca, and Natalie still tries not to blame her for it.

She did odd jobs growing up until she landed one that isn't so odd. She works at a call center where she's trained to coerce people to pay on their defaulted student loans. Everyone hates it there except Natalie. Natalie works the first shift so she's home by four and tells Mack all kinds of stories about the people she talks with.

"One guy had a cancer relapse at the beginning of the call, but once I told him about our payment plan, he was magically cured." Mack smirks and drinks iceless water from his whiskey glass. She knows he's still drinking because the countdown has begun. He'll be heading to the bar soon, and he never asks her to join him.

She could tell him to stay or she could even go with him. But she's not sure which one would be worse.

So she lets him go and hugs him, breathing in his showered scent. It's kind of like watching a part of yourself walk right out the door.

• • • •

NATALIE IS PROMOTED because she's a hard worker and makes it a habit to know everything about everything. Her manager is named Val, and she's beautiful and blonde but always walks around with a slight hangover; her hand seems permanently glued to her temple. Natalie tries not to think about where she was the night before, if she was at the bar and knows what Mack's been up to.

Natalie keeps rubbing those rocks and concentrates on the fact that she makes more money now. They can finally afford a house.

They move in over the weekend with Jaime's help. Rochelle offers to stop by with Glenn, but when she shows up she's Glenn-less and doesn't say a word about it. She helps Natalie sweep the floors and dust and start unpacking the boxes stacked up in the living room. It's a cute house: two bedrooms, wooden floors. It's secluded and stands guard off a gravel road.

Mack's outside with Jaime, saying their goodbyes. Rochelle looks at her, and it's a deep look that makes Natalie blink.

"I didn't do so great." She starts but then stops.

"What? When?" Natalie says, but she knows what Rochelle is saying.

"With Mack." Her eyes are rimmed with water, and I place my hand on her shoulder. "I wanted the wrong things because I thought they were the right ones." She sighs and lets the water wash her face. "All I'm asking..." She rubs at her cheek.

"It's okay," Natalie says even though she knows none of this is.

"All I'm asking is that you don't try to fix him. Don't put that on yourself. Only Jesus can do that." She pats at her cheeks to try and erase the evidence. Natalie nods but doesn't believe her. Natalie, she has a good heart. But she's convinced she's birthed that heart herself.

That night she takes a pregnancy test, and she knows there's a baby where the rocks should be. She imagines tiny toes fluttering inside her abdomen although it's way too early for that. She goes to tell Mack but waits for a moment in the bathroom. She relishes this one blink of time when it's just her and her daughter.

• • • •

HER STOMACH IS GROWING swollen, but that doesn't stop Val from asking her to the bar when she sees her in the break room. "It will be fun. For old times' sake." Val's talking about the one other time Natalie went with her, the night she met Mack. It's not as strange of an ask this time since Natalie is Val's team lead now and an official member of management. She places her hand on her belly, but Val doesn't seem to notice and frankly, doesn't care. Natalie figures the woman would drink with a wooden door if it came to it.

Mack doesn't protest. He's going to a poker game with Leon, and he's almost relieved that she won't be sitting on the couch while he's out with the boys. It's like Natalie sits on a ridge in his brain when he's out drinking even though she's convinced he doesn't think of her at all.

"Tonic, please," and the bartender brings her a sweaty glass of carbonated water while Val kicks back another Sex on the Beach. This is her second, and she's already had a shot of something that smelled like grapefruit.

"I love this. I love being young." Val smiles at herself, and Natalie tries not to notice her crow's feet. She's certain Val is at least thirty, and the most she knows about the woman is that she lives alone with two cats. And it's a shame, Natalie thinks, because someone who still has a little fire in her eyes should be with someone who loves her, should be married and making herself a home.

There's a loud commotion at the front of the bar. Mack comes in with a pack of noise and testosterone and Val perks up a bit. "The meat market's open for business," Val says and catches her balance when she hops off her stool. Natalie tries not to go too deep inside herself to lick the bitter taste of irony.

• • • •

WREN IS A WRINKLY PINK baby, and if Natalie had any friends, she'd brag about how she has to be smarter than all the other babies. Her eyes are always open and taking everything in from the lamb mobile shifting above her head to the feel of Mack's rough work shirt. She feels a closeness to her daughter that almost presents itself like an escape hatch. She finds herself thinking and talking about Wren like she made her with her own two hands and a thread of misunderstanding is sewn into the back of Natalie's mind.

Wren is not hers. Wren is mine.

"What if I'm a horrible father?" Mack says.

"Well, she's already here, and you've proven you're not." Nine months in and Rochelle is watching Wren for what she packages as "a much needed night off" for the new parents. But there is no night off for Natalie who feels her daughter in every labored movement. She pours hot water into a tea cup and sees her baby's face. The tea steeps and the timer goes off, and she can hear her cry in her ears. Mack is unaware of this tedious kind of existence, and Natalie tries not to feel superior in her head.

"What if I hurt her?" he whispers. She comes and sits next to him and puts the chamomile down on the coffee table. Mack puts his head on Natalie's shoulder, and she takes his shaky hand. She turns over the black-inked heart, palm facing up, and rubs the light white scar on his wrist like rubbing away his past. She doesn't know how a mother doesn't notice, and her hate burns hot for Rochelle. Rochelle who's watching her baby.

"Maybe we should go get her," Natalie goes to move off the couch, but Mack turns his head and kisses her. He kisses her so deeply that she can almost ignore the whiskey taste on his breath. She lets herself go for a minute and pretends the wall she's built between them is merely a pebble. But then the small clock on the side table ticks, and she thinks of Wren's beating heart.

• • • •

REBECCA HAS A BABY which changes things. They go from never talking anymore to talking all the time. They peck at their children like mother hens and visit their father's home that smells like cooking oil and tortillas even though his freezer is packed with microwavable meals. They play family again, and for an instant, Natalie pretends she's happy.

"I never thought it would happen. Five years trying and then out comes this one." Rebecca puts her face close to Antonio's whose hair is black and whispy and pokes out of his blue blanket. Natalie smiles at her. She takes some ownership of the woman Rebecca has become, frankly more than half, because it was her who put on Rebecca's shoes and made her lunches for the longest time. There's a soft stab when Natalie remembers the feel of her mother holding her in her arms.

"Well, that's amazing. He's a beautiful boy." Rebecca nods. It's late summer, the time before fall pretends to have any existence in this part of the country. They're sitting on their father's back stoop while their respective husbands grill out in the yard.

"You think Daddy's going to be okay?" Rebecca asks into the top of Antonio's head.

"Oh, yeah. The man's a beast. Nothing can stop him." Another soft stab when she remembers the way he cried all the way home from the hospital, baby Rebecca strapped in the back, motherless Natalie strapped in the front.

"Heart issues though. No good." Natalie nods and looks at the patio table they've already set. Guacamole and frijoles and the tortillas she fried earlier in the kitchen. The air smells like carne asada, and she feels like she's writing over her past with a red pen.

"Look at them. Look at our two manly men," Rebecca says, and Natalie looks at the two gringos they snagged, one at a bar, one at a church. "What good guys."

Natalie feels a pang of jealousy when she nods at the half-truth.

• • • •

WHEN WREN IS THREE, there's an incident. She finds a quart of whiskey barely buried in Mack's toolbox and carries it around with her like a baby doll. By the time Wren hits the side of the house where Natalie is raking leaves, she's played with the cap, and it comes off in her hand. Natalie smells the whiskey even before she sees her daughter. She turns, and there's a stain on Wren's shirt. She smacks away the bottle and grabs her, ignoring her gasp-like yelps. She sticks her fingers in her daughter's mouth, smells at her breath. Wren writhes silently, her face hot with anger.

"It's okay, baby. Let Mommy see." Natalie's voice is too panicky, and she watches Wren twist out of her arms and sit on the grass. She drinks in that moment like some of the other ones that bite at her skin.

Her daughter's back, bent over and tired and smelling of booze. She breathes in the tainted air and chucks the bottle hard against the house. She only notices Mack staring at her when Wren starts to cry.

• • • •

I GIVE HER ONE MORE moment because the last one is the tumor that's never stopped growing. There's an evening when Wren is over at Rebecca's, and Natalie is sitting on the floor in their living room. The wood is hard on her hips, but she hasn't been able to stop. It's the box in her lap, this box that holds so many different parts of a past she's only briefly been invited to. It's the box Mack keeps that they've never talked about. He's in bed—still hungover from the night before—and in some sick way, she thinks he owes her. So she starts to look through it like she's staking some sort of claim, but the feeling wears off when she holds Mack and Dennis in her hands. It's a picture of them standing in the street in front of Dennis's duplex, Mack's old home. They're two feet apart, Dennis's hands clasped against the front of him, Mack's to the side like they don't know where to go. She cries so hard, she kisses the floor and dust is washed with tears.

"What are you doing?" Mack's aglow in lamplight. He looks like he's let a series of trucks take a run at him.

"Um, I'm not–"

"Why are you looking at that?" His voice is gentle. In fact, there's almost a note of relief. Natalie knows his past. But now she gets to see it.

"I'm sorry. I just...I just want to know why." She starts crying again and digs her palms into her eyes. She feels his arms around her, and she feels comforted but also just as lost. She can't fix him. *Only Jesus can*, she hears in her head. She's so angry at that because she can barely understand what it means. She puts her arms around his waist and sticks her face into his neck.

"I'm sorry this happened to you," she says, and he holds her tighter.

• • • •

I PLACE MY HAND ON her back. She senses it's time. Time to get up. Time to face the music singing in the leaves. Time to hold her daughter and call 911. But she lingers for one more moment because it's hard to leave a past you never wanted in the first place.

Chapter Seven

Rochelle takes care of the arrangements. They use the funeral home Glenn Augustus's family has used for the extensive amount of members who have died from old age or drug overdose. Natalie's family, The Rojases, remain in a tight clump near the casket until Rebecca's husband, Steven, takes a screaming Antonio out in the foyer.

Mack's body is on display, all dried and dressed and a fine coat of makeup covers where his old face was. His button-down is buttoned all the way up. He looks like himself but not himself. Natalie wishes they would have closed the casket. But she was oddly thinking this would be a real goodbye.

In the pew, Rochelle sits at Natalie's left and is flanked on the other side by Glenn who puts on his public persona. He's cordial and is able to do the pleasantries while Natalie sits like a sack of potatoes against Rochelle. Rochelle has her arm around her, but the only things Natalie can feel are Wren's warmth and the quiet "daddies" floating from her mouth. Rebecca sits on the other side of Wren, husbandless, until Steven comes and sits back down with their son. Their father, Benito, sits in the pew behind them, his hand on Natalie's shoulder.

Look at what you did now, Mack, she thinks, and then she winces. Her heart doesn't blame him. Her heart blames her, but she doesn't like the way that tastes either.

She can hear Val come in before she sees her. She talks too loud, and her pantsuit is too tight, but she's comforting against the home's formal interior. I nudge Val a little bit until she sits in the pew behind Natalie, next to Benito, and whispers her condolences in her ear.

On the screen above their heads is a montage that quickly plays over and over because they could only scrounge together twenty photos of Mack, and he's smiling in less than half of them. One hardly counts because he's lifting Wren up to the camera and his face is hidden behind her suspended body. That's the only one Natalie can bear to look at.

"Father, husband, friend," says the pastor at the pulpit.

Liar, Natalie thinks but mainly about herself.

• • • •

"I KNOW THIS ISN'T THE best time." They're in Glenn Augustus's gigantic house eating from small plastic plates. Val is crunching on a celery stick which she wishes was poking out of a Bloody Mary. Her pantsuit is two shades lighter than navy blue. She's the jammed thumb in a room full of pinkies.

Val doesn't know me. Val will never know me because she loves herself too much. But Val is exactly who I need to write Natalie's ending.

"What are you talking about?" Natalie is holding her plate of untouched food at her stomach. They're in Glenn's dining room facing the front window. Underneath the tree out front sits Wren and stands Steven with Antonio. Wren keeps pointing up, and Steven follows the point of her finger.

"There's a job in White Smoke. Floor manager. My old boss is looking for someone. She asked me, but I said no. I like it here. But I told her about you."

"What's there to tell?" Southern Account Services gave her two weeks bereavement. Natalie's dreading the fourteen days she'll sit quietly with Wren, juggling her daughter's pain and her own. And there's something else itching at her. Something Rochelle's preacher had said at the gravesite. "May we all pray that Mack is with Jesus now," like it would take an act of God for Mack to end up somewhere good. Natalie doesn't realize that's always the point. It's just up to her to believe it.

Val sets her plate down on the bench seat under the window. She takes Natalie's shoulders in her hands and looks her in the face. "You are the best thing that's happened to me at SAS. I mean that. You don't know what a good TL does for a manager. You have a good head and show up to work and aren't afraid to take calls. You're a closer. And Natalie, you have an opportunity to do something big for her." Val lifts her chin at Wren who's talking at Steven with her hands again, telling him what she had seen hanging from her tree. "You're not going to make it on a TL's salary raising a kid. I'm guessing the life insurance won't hold you over for long." Natalie nods, keeping her lips stiff against the truth. There is no life insurance.

"I can't just move her to a new place. Where is White Smoke anyways?"

"Northwest Arkansas area. Tara, my old boss, says it's beautiful."

"I don't care if it's right on the beach. I can't move Wren away from her family."

"How are you going to survive?"

"I'll figure it out. I'll ask for a raise. Maybe Rochelle..." But she quickly puts a lid on the thought. She doesn't want to be a pity case, taking handouts. Plus, she doesn't want to gamble on how long Glenn's good nature would last.

"You already make more than the other TLs. And don't tell anyone I told you that. And they're not looking to grow management right now, Natalie. You know I'd vouch for you if I thought there was a chance." Val plants her hand against her temple. She drank enough this morning to get her through the funeral but her body is yelping at her now.

"I'll think about it," Natalie says, distracted by her daughter who is wide-eyed as she clasps her hands around her neck and flails out her feet. Then she sits back under the tree, her little play coming to a close.

· · · ·

NIGHTS ALONE ARE AGONY. I sleep at her side and watch her face struggle in exhausted sleep. And then she's awake again. She studies the ceiling, the blank space next to her. She wonders what ever happened to Todd Hiney and if it's too late to make amends. She feels guilty for thinking like this. But she feels all alone.

Maybe, I should take that job.

Wren walks in. She looks more like she's drifting in between Natalie's sleepy eyelids. She climbs into bed with her mother and Natalie holds her close to her heart. She smells like green apple bath bubbles. Natalie rubs her still damp hair against her cheeks. They have a silent conversation.

I miss Daddy.

Me, too.

And then they drift together.

. . . .

"YOU CAN'T. YOU CAN'T do this to me. To all of us."

Wren plays with her plastic tea set in her room, and Natalie concentrates on the sound of plastic attacking plastic. Rochelle is wearing black slacks and a white button down. Her frizzy hair is plastered back into a bun and there are pearls at her ears. She gives off the impression of a frazzled penguin and the thought piles on top of all the other worries and concerns in Natalie's chest.

"That's not what this is. I just have to think about Wren. Her future."

"Her future should include her family." Rochelle pats a chewed up Kleenex around her eyes. The iced sweet tea Natalie made has gone untouched and sweats in the overheated room. Texas winter is right outside the door, and even though it's only fifty-nine degrees outside, the two women feel ice cold on the inside.

"Dennis won't even return my calls. My son's dead. Now you're taking my granddaughter. What does your father think about this?"

"I'm calling him next." Rochelle smirks and shakes her head.

"You don't know what you're doing, Natalie. You're acting out of hurt. You don't have to run away." Rochelle speaks it to her daughter-in-law, but we both know she's talking to her old self. The scared girl who was raped and left for dead and ran away from a family who wouldn't have much to say on the matter even if they had known the truth. Except for Dennis. Sometimes, she wonders if she would have nailed down her feelings and just accepted whatever help they might have offered, if Mack would have turned out different. If she would have turned out different, too.

"Just, think about it for a while. Please. I'll be praying. I know God has this figured out, Natalie. Let us be there for you." Natalie's stomach sours when she thinks about me. I'm the one who did this to her if I even exist at all.

"Sure. Of course," Natalie says when Rochelle leans forward to hug her. She doesn't tell her mother-in-law that she already had the interview. That she's already got the job. That she's already put in her two weeks' notice. She just holds on tight to Rochelle, a quiet goodbye.

• • • •

REBECCA WON'T TALK to her. She slammed down the phone, and when Natalie called back, it was Steven's subdued voice telling her Rebecca wasn't feeling well. Natalie was so angry. She gave up what it meant to be a child just so Rebecca could know the feeling. And now she needs to go on and grow and all her sister can think about is the way it's going to affect her. It's like talking to Rochelle all over again.

She explains this to her father who just nods. They're sitting in his kitchen, Wren curled up and asleep in his lap. It's an unfair image, seeing what she knows could be fostered if she stayed in Texarkana. But it's also alarming, all these hands reaching out for Wren and elbowing her out of the picture.

She doesn't mean to think it. But she does.

"She's just sad, mija. She loves you and feels like you're abandoning her." His eyes betray him. They tell her he feels the exact same way.

"I'm not leaving because I don't love her. Or any of you. I just need to make sure life turns out okay even after...all this." She drags her hand across the air like a game show host.

"The foolishness of man perverteth his way: and his heart fretteth against the Lord," Benito whispers into Wren's ear. Everyone calls him Benny and sees a wise old face when they meet him. But Benny isn't old, really. Mid-fifties but a lifetime has come and curled up inside of him. His wife, Angela, was how he navigated point A to point B. She had told him that verse when he was a young man and dead set on moving heaven and earth for her. And she reminded him, as she often did in her gentle way, that he just wasn't that powerful. And maybe that was a good thing.

"I don't, I don't know what that means, Daddy." Natalie feels real grief warm her skin and the tears behind her eyes. It's a strong reaction to hearing my Word and her heart and head fretting against it. There's a soft feeling against her chest, like a balled up fist lightly striking her sternum, but she digs her fingers into her face and ignores it.

"Not now, mija. But some day," Benny says and places Wren back into her arms.

• • • •

SHE PACKS ALONE FOR a while, a pick ax playing with her temple. She puts memories and old jokes and a million tears and not enough laughs into boxes while Wren goes and plays at her tree. She thought about telling her to stop. To stay inside. But she knows Wren wouldn't listen because all she wants is to stand under it and look up above.

The moving truck comes. She had finally gotten Rebecca on the phone and they had a somewhat civil conversation, but she doesn't plan on coming by. Rochelle doesn't either. Wren spent the night with her last night, and when Natalie went to pick her back up, Glenn claimed Rochelle had a headache. Her father did show up early on his way to work. He kissed her forehead and gave Wren a big hug. He gave Natalie her mother's old crucifix that he put in her palm. She was shocked it didn't burn her skin.

I stand shoulder to shoulder with her as the phone rings. She's surprised to hear Glenn's voice.

"Hey, uh, Natalie. You have a moment?" She nods and forgets herself, spits out a "sure." One of the movers is carrying Mack's box of photos, and her heart twists itself into a knot.

"We received word that Dennis is dead." She looks outside, and Wren has grabbed the tree's waist as she sings and dances around it.

"What–how? When?"

"We found out a few hours ago. A neighbor...a neighbor smelled something and called the police. It looks like he was strangled. Natalie?"

"Yes?"

"They think it was Mack."

"Mack? What do you mean?" She can hear Wren's song coming through the windows now, her stuffed dog, Roy, a patient audience.

"They think he did it. There was no forced entry. Didn't he stop by to check on him the night...you know. Didn't he mention Rochelle called and asked him to see if Dennis was okay?" All the thoughts in Natalie's mind are playing a massive game of hide and seek. She tries to catch them and sit them down, look them in the face. But they're too quick for her.

"No. I mean, I guess I really don't know. He wouldn't do that. He would never...that's not Mack." Knowing the history doesn't help. She shuts her eyes against everything. She doesn't need her daughter to know her father was a murderer, too.

"Look, it'd be a posthumous trial, and since Rochelle is Dennis's next of kin, she can make the call on whether or not she wants to look into it. But she's obviously not going to. She wanted to call you herself, but she can't think or talk really. She's devastated. I know you understand." His voice is soothing, and Natalie assumes it's the particular one he handpicks to calm down his clients.

"Okay. That's good, I guess. I'm leaving, Glenn. Like here soon. I imagine she doesn't want me to drop by."

"No, she's a mess right now. I'm sure she'll make plans to visit in person once you're settled."

"Yeah, okay. Look, I need to go. Thank you," she says, which feels weird to say. "Thank you for ruining my life even more" is what she feels like saying. But it isn't Glenn's fault. It's obviously Mack's.

She hangs up, and I put my arm around her. There's a bottom to all of this, and it feels sharp under bare feet. But I already know it's not sharp enough yet to turn her heart, so she uses the pain to hone in on the only thing that will matter to her for a while. We both watch Wren hug Roy and put her face into his threadbare fur.

Chapter Eight

Two years is not enough time to forget. There's never enough time for that. But Natalie tucks her past into her purse each morning before scanning her badge and walking to her desk. She locks it up in the attached filing cabinet where she keeps her pens and sticky notes. She clocks in and puts on her headset and pretends she likes her manager, Herman, who smells slightly of tuna fish even first thing in the morning, and his boss, Tara McMahon who stands in her doorway and scans the collectors each time she's itching to fire one. Natalie hasn't been called in except for that one time. It's a tiny prayer to no one when she can see Tara stalking her office through the window that faces the collection floor. It's a sigh of relief when she closes the blinds.

Two years is also not enough time to forgive herself. She talks to so many people on the phone, and sometimes, she wonders what would happen if she stopped discussing their past due student loans and started talking about her dead husband instead. "He was a murderer and killed himself, but he gave our daughter a really cute stuffed dog, so it's not all bad." She laughs under her breath.

"Are you laughing?"

"No, sorry, just coughed for a second. Forgot to hit the cough button. I apologize. So how would you like to settle this amount today? We take credit cards and you can also send in a certified check by mail." She catches Herman out of the corner of her eye who nods at her and moves on down the aisle.

Two years is also more than enough time to get demoted. In fact, Natalie somehow managed to beat that record and was demoted within the first six months of moving to White Smoke. Nobody told her how hard it would be to meet collection goals. She could never get the right number of people to pay up. She could never get the big cash settlements. She couldn't even groom her team to be a cohesive working unit, and instead, was training a tiny island of misfit toys who seemed to hate each other. And so there was that one day when Tara called her in and chewed her up. Spit her out. And she landed back as a TL, this time for a manager named Herman Salinas who seemed like the type to keep a lock on his basement door.

Lunchtime rolls around, and she's already exhausted by the manager call she had to take while Herman embarked on his daily fifteen-minute bathroom break.

"Heartbreak Herman killed his time this morning. Only thirteen minutes in the john. New record," Mary says. In spite of herself, Natalie has made a friend, Mary Zinberg. Mary is all eye shadow and teased hair. Big words, big personality. But she also cuts her skin, the inside of her upper arm. Her husband doesn't trust her and she hates being a mother to Rhonda, a former preemie who decided it just wasn't her time to die. Rhonda's spirit is all light, jammed-packed inside a six-year-old's body. I can't say the same for her mother. But Natalie likes her if only because Mary seems relatively normal at work and has a daughter the same age. Two years is plenty of time to find a good friend. Unfortunately, for Natalie, she's dropped the ball.

"Hang out tonight?" Natalie nods. She wants to shake her head "no," but she doesn't like being alone. There's a young man she refers to as a "creeper stoner" who lives with his grandfather across the hall and a Laotian family on her left that's always screaming at each other. Her plan was to save up enough in two years to put a down payment on something or at least find a house to rent. But her demotion has set her back. A lot of things have set her back.

She goes back to work and hears sob story after sob story, and it all mixes up with her own emotions. She takes a smoke break—a bad habit she's picked up from Mary—and stands alone in the rain because Mary's break is after hers. There are a few employees huddled under the umbrellaed benches near the dumpster but she stays put inhaling and trying to remember what Mack's face used to look like.

Five rolls around. There are no early shifts at Johnson Credit Collections, just the five and the six, so she's stuck piling out with a herd of sheep, as she likes to think of them. She nods goodbyes and keeps her face flat. She gives Mary a half hug and tells her she'll see her later on. In the Pinto, she finally opens her purse where she stores her past and takes out one of her tiny bottles of vodka.

In two years, a lot of things can change.

• • • •

THEY ALL WANT HER TO come back home to Texarkana even though she convinces them she's management, poised for a promotion. Her family doesn't believe her. *Fine*, she thinks and takes a swig.

She's on her way to Little Chicks to pick up Wren. She quickly downs the bottle and throws it into the glove compartment. At a red light, she one-eyes traffic as she reaches deeper in the compartment for gum and a bottle of cheap body spray. She chews and pollutes the air with fake flowers. The booze starts to kick in.

She blames Mack, of course. Why wouldn't she? She was his sounding board, the person who dug him out of the deep. But he wouldn't stop diving in, head first. She glances up at the rearview mirror, checks her mascara. One eye's smudged, and she uses a shaky finger to fix it. She looks again and wishes mirrors didn't exist.

She's a little late again and the lady at the front desk gives her a terse smile because of it. She signs in and goes to look for Wren. She finds her seated near the backpacks while two other stragglers rake their fingers through a bin of plastic bricks.

"Hey, there." Wren looks up, and her eyes are damp full moons. She begins to cry and Natalie hugs her, hoping she smells like anything but vodka. "What happened, baby?" Ms. Melanie edges in and introduces her entrance with sneakers against linoleum. Ms. Melanie is small, young, and blonde and far less nice than she looks.

"Kids being kids. It started on the van ride from school. One of the kids asked about her daddy. They started making fun of her. You know how these things go."

"No, I don't," Natalie says, the vodka in her stomach making her brave. "Which kid?"

"Not sure. The driver wasn't aware of what was going on." *How convenient,* Natalie thinks. She starts to say so, but the fluorescent lights above starburst. She closes her eyes until the fireworks display calms down.

"Are you okay?" Ms. Melanie asks. Natalie shakes her head "yes," stricken mute with fear. *Get it together, Natalie.*

"I'll talk to Wren," is all she can manage to say. Because in spite of her daughter's pain, Little Chicks is the cheapest after school program in town. And also in spite of Wren's pain, the world is cruel, and Natalie knows there's absolutely nothing she can do about it.

• • • •

THEY EAT. STORE BOUGHT macaroni and cheese and broccoli fresh from the microwave. They've already eaten the meat she's bought with her food stamps. She watches Wren. Waits for her to say anything. But she eats her slow bites and doesn't let on that she doesn't have a father when all the other kids do.

After dinner is Wren's bath. Natalie sits on the toilet, head in her hands, trying to figure out how to say something, anything about what happened, but she spirals down the dark tunnel in her head. It's the most pronounced it's ever been, and the demon on her shoulder bares his teeth at me. I could pluck him with two fingers or simply flick him against the ceiling, but I don't. I let her have this moment.

"Can we talk about what happened?" Natalie asks in her best mom voice. She wipes at her face with a shaky hand and looks at Wren in the tub. She hasn't changed out of her pantsuit she picked up free of charge from Women Who Work in exchange for sitting through a few seminars and one-on-ones. Her contact, Francesca, still calls her from time to time but Natalie has a knack for pretending the phone doesn't exist. She sniffs at the second hand suit and feels like she's brining in her own sweat.

"What happened?" Wren asks. But Natalie notes the edge.

"What your friend said. About Daddy."

"She's not my friend. She's a stupid face."

"We don't say that."

"Then tell her not to be mean." Wren tucks her chin against her chest and stops playing in the bubbles. Natalie crawls her fingers through her daughter's wet hair like a trembling spider.

· · · ·

SHE TUCKS WREN IN WITH Roy and plants a kiss on her forehead. She should have said more, maybe told her daughter how sorry she was and how unfair everything turned out to be. But all she can think about is the cold vodka in the freezer and the taste of forgetting.

When the doorbell rings, she finds Mary in her fluffy pink pajamas and bunny slippers. Only Mary would wear her pajamas outside, in the rain.

"Cats and dogs," Mary says although it's only a light drizzle. Natalie has already started the night off with a double shot which no longer has the same kick it used to. But she's in a good mood because she has the whole night and the whole bottle. Just enough to forget how rough everything feels to the touch.

Mary cracks open her own pint of whiskey and finds a glass in one of the cabinets. Mary's got it nice. Her husband's still alive and she has her own curly headed six-year-old at home. The envy is so sharp beneath Natalie's skin that she doesn't even stop to think why Mary isn't home with them.

"To us ladies. May we drink away the worry, slay away the men, and take any– and everything we want!" Mary drinks her glass dry, and Natalie tips back another double. I see the dark shadow at her shoulder, small but still there. It bares its teeth as I shine my light.

• • • •

MARY IS TRANSFERRED to Natalie's team. Over the past few weeks, Natalie has clocked in early and has been attentive to Herman's every ask. She even declogged one of the toilets when he pawned the job off on her.

"I don't get why this place doesn't have a janitor."

"Why pay a janitor when you can have an hourly slave do the job?" Mary inhales her Marlboro and puffs out a cloud with pursed lips. Natalie tries the same move, but she feels like she looks like a puffer fish.

"What's happening on the stud front? And don't say 'I'm not ready.' I'm not saying you have to settle down with someone. Just have a little fun. You're twenty-eight for goodness sakes, Nat! You deserve to live a little." Natalie almost chokes on another smoke cloud. She could very easily argue she's lived a lifetime.

"I don't know. The only places I go are here, Little Chicks, and the apartment." She gazes out at the picnic tables crawling with JCC employees. "Slim pickings in my opinion."

"Yeah, well, if I had your freedom, I'd be picking my way across the country, slim or not."

"Mary, you barely make any sense."

Mary smiles. "Girl, I haven't made sense since the seventies."

• • • •

ONE NIGHT, MARY COMES over and takes out a little vial. "This. This will loosen you up."

"I didn't think I needed loosening." They sit in Natalie's tiny living room, feet curled up on the sofa. It's still the same couch she used to sit on with Mack. She watches Mary dump a little straight on the coffee table with the broken leg. As she snorts a line, all Natalie can see is Nancy Reagan's disappointed face.

"It's the nineties," Natalie says. "We should know better."

"We should probably do a lot of things," Mary says.

Mary nods at the powder she's poured for Natalie. How nice it would be, she thinks, to inhale and let go. To forget the past ever existed and to not have to pay for her sins each excruciating minute.

She starts to dive forward when her eyes catch two naked feet pointing at her from the hallway.

"Mommy, I'm scared," Wren says, but it's Natalie's heart that takes the beating.

• • • •

"DOES GREG KNOW?" NATALIE asks. They're at the mall sitting on a sticky bench while the girls waste quarters riding mechanical animals.

"Know what? Poor Greg barely knows what day it is," Mary says. Her eyelids are a hot shade of pink, matching her cheeks and lips. Natalie is physically prettier, but there's a small rope of doubt connecting her thoughts to the truth. Her tiny demon swings on it.

"About, you know. The drugs?" After Wren came in, Natalie asked Mary to leave. It was the panic in her chest that kicked her friend out of her apartment, not Natalie herself. She didn't like the feel of it or the way Mary looked at her in her fluffy pajamas, carefully scooping the white powder back into its tiny vial. She didn't like the accusing face Mary gave her, which is why Natalie asked her to meet at the mall.

"Oh, Natalie. You're so adorable." Mary carefully hides her bitterness, but the demon turns Natalie's thoughts towards it. She feels ashamed of accusing her friend. "It's just enough to loosen up a little. I'm not a drug addict or anything." Natalie looks into her friend's face, studies the rainbows painted on her eyelids. "And Greg?" Mary says, getting up to pry Rhonda off of a very purple Dino. "He thinks what I tell him to."

• • • •

MARY'S STANDOFFISH for a couple of days, to the point that Natalie eats in her car and people watches during lunch. She comes around eventually though, even chatting Natalie up at her desk before they clock in for the morning.

Natalie starts to notice things she doesn't want to. Like how close Mary stands to Herman and how she's no longer wearing her wedding ring on her left hand. When Natalie's alone at night watching Johnny Carson, she takes big gulps of her vodka and tries to un-pluck the thoughts that won't stop weaving together. Mary is hurting herself. And she's going to hurt her family.

Natalie repeats it to herself like a mantra without ever looking in the mirror.

• • • •

"WHY DID IT TAKE YOU so long to get back to me?" Rebecca is cry-talking, and it hurts Natalie's ear. She's been avoiding calling back her sister who left a dire "we need to talk" message on her answering machine a few days ago. She makes the call on her break at the pay phone near JCC's front entrance.

"I didn't, I mean–"

"He died, Natalie."

"Who?" But she already knows.

"Dad."

"But...how?"

"His heart. His heart gave out." *The foolishness of man perverteth his way: and his heart fretteth against the Lord,* Natalie thinks. She's still snatching at each word floating in front of her when Rebecca says, "So, can you make it?" Natalie's spaced but she finally gets what Rebecca's saying.

"Oh, when is it?"

"Tomorrow. 6 PM."

"Rebecca, you know there's no way–"

"Oh, I know. But I just wanted to hear you say it. I just wanted to hear you say you're not going to Dad's funeral because you're too self-absorbed to call me back. Because you're living your dream life in nowheresville Arkansas. Does it taste good, Natalie?"

"What? Does what taste good?" ...*and his heart fretteth against the Lord.*

"Swallowing your own B.S."

• • • •

SHE DOESN'T TELL WREN about Abuelo. In fact, she doesn't tell herself about her father's death, opting to file it in the Z's and throw away the key. She worries, though, that she's mentioned her father to Mary before and that some sort of situation will arise where she'll casually mention her father's death and Mary will be disappointed Natalie never told her. Mary seems to be the core of Natalie's thoughts lately, but Natalie's too busy worrying about Mary to notice.

The demon follows her to work. It's grown, and its stench suffocates the office. Natalie washes her thoughts away with big splashes of flowery body spray, but her co-workers can smell it on her. Something's happening.

Mary tells her she has a hair appointment that evening. "Sometimes, I don't get home until ten. The perm takes forever but Sadie likes to split a bottle of wine, and we shoot the breeze. I'm blessed to have a friend like her." It snags at Natalie like it's meant to. But the other side of her brain is consumed with the fact that Mary won't be home after work.

They say their goodbyes, and Natalie's heart overworks inside her chest. I sit next to her, and in the back sits a man that's not a man, his body bathed in light. On the roof of her car is the demon, its nails tapping a noxious tune as we turn into traffic. Her hand goes for her bottle deep inside her purse. She drinks the small bottle like Alice does in Wonderland, but instead of shrinking like Alice, her body goes numb, except for her shaky hands. Like Alice, she drowns in her own tears.

"Mack!" she screams as she soars down the freeway. She's free-associated Mack as the root of her problem, which means she's digging up the wrong tree. The man that's not a man puts his hand on her shoulder, and now it's just tears she can barely see through–no more noise.

We turn into a neighborhood where a cluster of houses that all look alike sit on a cul-de-sac. This isn't the first time Natalie's been here. She looked up Mary's address weeks ago, sometimes driving a sleeping Wren to Mary's house. She has to drive slowly and sometimes with one eye, but I haven't allowed her decisions to catch up with her just yet.

She pulls up tentatively, her front tire making friends with the curb. She wishes she had more vodka. She pumps more body spray and singes the inside of her mouth with peppermint. She's going to be late picking up Wren, so she shoots more Binaca into her mouth to punish herself. After she's brushed through her hair and smoothed Carmex over her lips, she gets out of the car and walks to the front door.

"Hello?" Greg Zinberg is as small as she imagined he'd be. Khaki pants and a brown sweater over his button down. He's a beaten-down version of this morning's Greg who keeps mantras in his back pocket in the hopes of conquering high school hormones and passive threats from the superintendent. "You need to take a hard line stance against the enemy, Greg. You go weak at the most inopportune times." *Have you been talking to my wife*? ran through Greg's head. And then the tired chuckle nobody else could hear.

"Hi. I'm...I'm Natalie."

"Oh? Natalie? Oh, Mary's friend."

"Yes." She wishes it were raining so he'd hurry her inside. But Greg doesn't look like the type to hurry. He keeps the door tight against him, afraid to open his space to the outside.

"Mary's not here right now."

"I know. I'm actually here to talk to you."

"Me?" Greg asks. He pales even though Natalie's in no way threatening. But there is something palpable about her, me, and the man that's not a man behind her on the right, the demon on her left. It's fingering the collar of her shirt.

"It's about Mary. I think she has a drug problem." Natalie waits for it to register, but what she doesn't understand is how tethered Greg is to the here and now. Nothing can change. Nothing can get any worse.

"You have the wrong person or you're up to something. I need you to leave or I'll call the cops." Greg is having an out of body experience, and his fear propels the last line. Natalie recognizes the mistake she's made, and the demon smiles even though it can hear the sizzle of its own skin. "And do yourself a favor, stop ruining your life. I know a drunk when I see one," he says and softly closes the door in Natalie's face.

· · · ·

THE DAY MARY CONFRONTS Natalie during first break is the day she's promoted to TL. Herman claims the team is growing and there's nothing wrong with needing two of them. Mary gloats about it and eagerly eats one of the breakfast donuts Herman brings in to celebrate. Natalie smiles even though she's still nursing a terrible hangover. She tries her best to hit her call count so she doesn't have to talk to Mary.

At break time, Mary nods her head at her, and Natalie follows her out into the front parking lot. There's a terrible deadening she nurses in her belly as she trails Mary to her Taurus. Natalie gets into the passenger side. Inside, it smells like Aquanet.

"I'm so happy you got to meet my husband." Natalie stares into the windshield, watches the Taiwanese man who owns the donut shop sweep near the front door.

"Look–"

"No. No, Natalie, you look." And Natalie does. Today, Mary is wearing green across her lids and a very pale purple lip gloss. Her bangs are crimped and arc across her forehead. "I get that you're jealous. I get that you want what I have, but if you ever step foot near my home again, I swear I will get a restraining order against you. And drugs? Seriously? What are we? In sixth grade? You couldn't keep your mouth shut and just enjoy the moment, could you?" Mary snags hers fingers through her crunchy hair. "I get it now."

Natalie's chin presses towards her chest. "Get what?"

"Your life. Your husband. Why everything crashes down so hard around you. You're a bulldozer, Natalie. You're the kind of person that just shouldn't be touched." Mary gets out of the car. Natalie nods at the windshield as she watches her go back inside.

• • • •

THERE WAS ONE PERFECT day with just the three of them. It was a long weekend–Memorial Day–so they decided to go to Galveston. The beach was crammed and they felt like sardines sitting on the shoreline, but happy sardines. Mack would run into the water with a screaming two-year-old Wren on his hip. Natalie sat in the sand, her toes digging into it to feel the coolness underneath. She was reading a book, and when she thinks of it, she keeps whispering to her dream self, "Look up. Look up." And when she does, she sees her past, her present, her future. The two people who made anything worth anything. But then she looks down and starts reading again.

The hotel room, dinner on the beach, the way she felt in Mack's arms once Wren was asleep. These are all there, too, surrounding her like a gull in her ear or the crash of ocean water against her shins. But the sharpest part is always the moment she looks up, and the sun has set them on fire.

She's choking on memory and some of the vodka she's swallowed. She's graduated from the tiny bottles in her purse to putting some in a plastic water bottle she keeps in her car. She takes tentative sips during break time and lunch, not wanting to overdo it but wanting to do enough. She's tired of Mary's face. She's tired of Mary's spineless husband. She's tired of feeling defeated.

She's tired of herself.

Natalie blinks away the thought because she's on her way to pick up Wren from Little Chicks. She's scrounged together enough change for ingredients to bake cookies for the weekend. She just wants to be in her PJs with Wren. She wants to hug her and smell her hair. She wants to sit on the couch and close her eyes and remember what the ocean and laughter sound like.

But her thoughts butterfly away when the car in front of her slams on its breaks. She tests out hers in the Pinto, but it's too slow on the uptake, and she ends up rear-ending the Bronco in front of her. Her head lurches forward and then hits hard against the headrest. She's spinning through butterfly wings of thought until an officer pulls up and directs her to get out of the car. The EMT shows up, and as she's inspected and handled like a broken vase, she thinks of that other moment, when her face was out of her book, and her husband, her daughter sat with her as the sun went down. And how it was a beautiful moment but also a little bit scary, the way the light could slowly sink away.

She takes a breathalyzer test. The cop won't answer her when she asks about the Bronco owner who's strapped down onto a gurney and maneuvered into the ambulance. She's cuffed and watched by a pretty, younger officer while the other one searches her car and malls through her purse. She knows he won't find any more bottles in there, but she's surprised by what he does find. A tiny vial of coke.

Natalie starts to panic and screams that it isn't hers. She shoulders off the younger cop and moves toward the other officer, but she's told to stop and get on the ground. She's forced there by a knee in the middle of her back, her cheek kissing gravel. Her mind is a movie screen and all she can see is Wren's beautiful face.

Belly and breast against ground, I touch her hair, and I whisper comfort in her ear. But she drowns in the sound of ocean waves and the ghosts of those who can't save her.

Chapter Nine

Eye through glass, Rochelle sees the tree her granddaughter sat against two years ago. It was during her son's funeral, after she trailed her daughter-in-law and that terrible woman, Val, into the library. They left, shoulder-to-shoulder, co-conspirators in the biggest hurt Rochelle had felt in a very long time. But at that point, it just looked like Natalie was taking comfort in a wayward co-worker and her granddaughter was resting against a tree.

But things aren't always what they seem. At least that's what her therapist, Dr. Neese, says.

It's the one thing we agree on.

Dennis. Dennis always saunters in, even more so than Mack. But really, the two are forever intertwined in Rochelle's head and heart. Two different sides of the same problem. She was too busy to help them. Too busy to fix them.

You can't fix a person, I whisper in her ear, and she nods at the tree through the glass.

"I know. I know that's your job. But you can imagine why I'm slightly disappointed." She smiles, and the tear slides over her upper lip. *I know*, I say. And she touches her chest where she hears me say it.

"The worst part is Wren. I can't help her. I mean, I can't watch you help her." Rochelle fits inside her new self like a pair of too tight pants. She feels constricted. She acknowledges the concept of freedom. The letting go and letting me. But her heart clings onto her old understanding of the world. One foot in, one foot out. She doesn't even have the courage to tell Glenn she got baptized.

"I didn't do so well." It's the same song she plays on rotation that she refuses to erase. "Mack needed me. I gave him so little." Another tear traces the other side of her face. She pretends she's watching her granddaughter dance beneath the tree. "He needed me, and I traded him for a castle and a dream." The library's A/C starts up overhead, and Rochelle feels her bony arms through her sweater.

"Who are you talking to?" Glenn comes in. He's tugging a white hand towel around his neck. Glenn is flourishing. He's fifty-five and looks in his prime although every year for Glenn has been inarguably prime-worthy. At least that's the way it's spun when Rochelle feels her weakest. She's lost weight. Her face has thinned. There are lines where youth once lived. Glenn doesn't make her pay for it, though. He still kisses her hairline like he does now, and she's just about to tip into the depth of love she has in her heart for him when she stops herself. The air blows cold at the top of her head, and she looks up.

"Nobody," she says, the truth too strange to say out loud.

• • • •

AS CHILDREN, THEY LOOKED more alike. Twins. Rochelle didn't tell anyone how strange it made her feel. Here was someone who was half her and half himself. Someone who by all intents and purposes should have thought her thoughts and felt her feelings. But from the very beginning, Rochelle knew Dennis wasn't anything like her.

His thoughts were very different.

It started with the cats. Dead ones everywhere. Half buried in the bushes, hiding beneath the coiled garden hose. Each demise was orchestrated differently as if someone was adeptly practicing the art of killing. Their father assumed it was Pete Grisholm, the competing insurance adjuster in Wake Village. But their mother knew better.

She brought the priest out twice, both times when their father wasn't home. Their father, Bradford, already didn't like Dennis. He favored Rochelle although it was a lukewarm attempt at fatherly love. He was more the hunting and fishing type. Any verb, really, that got him out of the house.

Their mother, Eileen, loved them both but spent the majority of her time worrying about her son. It's the reason why in pictures, her eyes always looked pinched together, like the nerve between her eyebrows didn't know when to take the day off.

Bradford and Eileen were always surface deep with each other. To their friends, they were the perfect couple because they never fought. But that was only because it required an energy neither thought to waste on the other.

"I'm not sure how to help, Eileen. He won't tell me anything. He never says anything alarming in confession. He seems like a good boy." The priest was at the seat of honor on their pepto-pink couch. Their mother sat in the wingback chair next to it. The nerve looked like a worm dancing above the bridge of her nose.

"What about an exorcism?" This was the second visit and the second time she proposed it. Father Ward gave the same dumbfounded expression he did the first. "Fine," Eileen said. "Fine," she whispered but the worm didn't stop.

Rochelle heard every word because she was sitting under the dining room table. She eavesdropped a lot but never worried about getting in trouble, a byproduct of nobody ever worrying about her.

"We could do it ourselves," Rochelle said later after dinner. She dried the dishes as her mother dipped and wiped each one with a rag.

"Do what?" Eileen asked. She was like Rochelle, not particularly pretty but not ugly either. They each found themselves to be blendable, the type of person that could easily disappear in a crowd.

"The exorcism." Rochelle was eleven and barely knew what the word meant. But she had an unfailing confidence that she could do it. At eleven, she believed she could do anything.

"Oh, don't be ridiculous," Eileen said, but for an instant the worm stopped dancing.

"What happens during an exorcism?" Rochelle asked. She rubbed the plate in her hands and tried to see her face in it.

"Depends I guess. But the priest uses holy water and says some things in Latin. Sometimes they have to tie them up."

"Tie who up?"

Eileen stopped dipping and wiping to weave a finger into her beehive. She rolled the two words around in her mouth like marbles before offering them to her daughter. "The afflicted."

• • • •

AT THIS POINT, ROCHELLE and Dennis still shared a room. Dennis slept in the twin bed near the window and Rochelle slept in the one against the bare wall. His wrists were so small. A puny kid who didn't eat enough meat and poked at his vegetables. When his breathing turned rhythmic, Rochelle removed the laces from her Chuck Taylors. Dennis helped her out by sleeping with his arms raised upward like a swinging chimpanzee. She lightly laced each wrist to his bed posts, careful not to wake him. She figured his legs would be fine, and if things get out of hand, she'd jump on top of him.

She took the glass of water off her nightstand and dunked her fingers in it. She started waving them at Dennis and a spray of droplets hit his face. "Inyay ethay amenay ofyay esusjay ebay ongay atansay," Rochelle said in Pig Latin. It would be a vicious scene to anyone who came in and didn't know Rochelle's heart. It would look cruel, unnecessary. But Rochelle had a deep affinity for Dennis, and even though he was different, she realized he didn't have to be. If only she could fix him.

"What are you doing?" Dennis's eyes widened when he realized he couldn't move his arms. "Ro, why are you doing this? Let me go!" He tugged and his panic was loud in her ears. She untied his wrists, and he scooted up, bringing his knees to his chest.

"You're mean," he said, and when he said it, she knew what all those dead cats felt like.

It would become a thing she'd laugh about years later, before the rape when Rochelle still laughed. How silly to tie someone up and force the demons out. How silly to try and make someone different by sheer intent. And she'd look into Dennis's face when she said it only to see him not laughing.

• • • •

WHEN ROCHELLE WAS TWELVE and got her period, they moved Dennis to the basement. There was an undercurrent of meaning with that move, but everyone pretended it was okay to stuff a boy where you couldn't see him. Even Rochelle, Dennis's other half, began to forget about him. She was too wrapped up in telephoning her friends or reading about Bob Dylan in *Tiger Beat* to remember she had a brother.

She painted her room pink and mopped the floors, erasing any trace of the skinny boy in the bed next to her. Sometimes she'd pass the basement door and hear music trickling up the stairs and remember somebody was down there.

They stopped finding cats.

Eileen gave up worrying as a pastime; she, too, forgot what she couldn't see anymore. And once the cats were gone, her head went on a permanent vacation, pretending she was married to Dean Martin and living where she could hear the ocean.

Nobody thought to ask themselves what had replaced the cats.

• • • •

AT SEVENTEEN, ROCHELLE was far less blendable. She stood out, her long legs shown off in short shorts. She was the lucky one because her father never told her to cover up like the other girls' dads. Her mother's worm came back around this time but she never said anything either. She was tired of talking and nobody listening.

Rochelle wasn't popular but she was good looking enough that she had dates on the weekend. Sometimes double dates to the movies where she was pawed at in the backseat. Sometimes at the overlook where she was pawed at in the front. Rochelle never had any real qualms about this because it was the rite of passage everyone had to go through. So even though her good heart still beat in her chest, sometimes it would close its eyes at the worst moments.

Eventually, Rochelle got a reputation.

"They think you're a slut," Dennis said one day at the breakfast table. Her mother was flipping pancakes and her shoulder blades kissed when Dennis said it. Rochelle waited, silently begged her mother to say something, anything, but she continued to flap the jacks even with her shoulders pinched together.

"No they don't," Rochelle said. Her words were as weak as the coffee she doctored with cream and sugar. She had been having a hard time sleeping, sometimes the things she did with boys creeping into her dreams. She reasoned her aversion away, attempting to believe the sickness inside of her was like a meddling housewife who had no right to nose into her business.

"Yeah, they do. I'm just glad no one knows we're related."

"Me, too. For obvious reasons," Rochelle said, looking Dennis dead in the eye. He showed off his middle finger behind their mother's back and grabbed his books to leave. Rochelle had gone out of her way at school to keep Dennis's existence a private matter. And Dennis never cared to thwart her efforts.

Rochelle looked at her mother's back, burning holes into the Peter Pan collar at her neck. But Eileen kept looking out the window above the sink, wondering why everything bad had to happen to her.

• • • •

SOMETIMES, DENNIS GOT beat up. It wasn't unusual to see his lip puffed up or his nose out of joint. Their mother tried to drag him to their pediatrician, Dr. Willard, with the lollipops and phony smile. But Dennis shrugged off her good intentions and instead, let the pain consume him until it became his only good friend.

It was just by happenstance that the same guy who had punched Dennis in the face after school on October 14, 1965 was the same one who raped Rochelle later that night. Ricky Dean. Ricky's fight was always inside of himself. He had no one to blame. His parents had good hearts and more than enough love to go around, but Ricky refused to believe them. He wanted to test the waters, dip a toe over the edge. He became violent, finding Dennis—the weird kid from Spanish class—an easy target. And then he became even more violent when he noticed someone like Rochelle.

Easy prey.

Ricky would eventually see prison, see beatings far worse than ones he'd ever delivered. He'd sit shoulder to shoulder with a cinderblock wall and hyperventilate while holding a tiny Bible one of the Gideons had left the warden. He'd give himself over to me and look at his sins from time to time like a mirror. And then he'd break the glass.

"Kiss me," Ricky said. Rochelle was planted against the grass of somebody's side yard. She had been walking home from the library one of those rare dateless nights when she got to be nobody but herself. She had felt him before she heard him. He was up behind her, and his hand covered her mouth. He forced her between the houses—a bold move. His hand tasted like dried sweat. He was kissing her face even after he had done the deed, and she felt like hell would have been a nice respite. Just as quickly as he was planted on top of her, he was ripped off like a dirty bandage. She looked up at the hand attached to the skinny wrist gripping Ricky's collar.

Dennis.

I made Dennis do something different that night. He should have been holed up in his room, hitting the back of his head against his wall or drawing dark images until the paper tore. But I whispered a desire in his heart to take a walk. He figured it was to grow closer to the night or some nonsense like that. Really, it was to save his sister because Ricky wouldn't have stopped at the rape.

"Dennis, Dennis." Rochelle couldn't figure out if it was a question or not. She was just aware that her brother was mauling Ricky in the moonlight, and she didn't know how to make him stop. Or if she even wanted to.

A deck light popped on. An "Anyone out there?" traveled the length of the backyard to Rochelle's left.

"Dennis, come on," Rochelle said definitive, declarative. She grabbed his arm, and they ran all the way home.

Before they went in, he stopped her. He looked at her. Her hair was a mess and her top, untucked. She shifted her miniskirt down, and she was sure she was bleeding between her legs. But Dennis touched her lightly with the same hand that left Ricky unconscious in a yard two streets over.

"Ro, nobody can hurt you anymore," he said, well meaning but very wrong.

• • • •

DENNIS BECAME HER PROTECTOR. He'd been looking for a reason he was so alone and angry in this world, and then it was like he finally found his purpose. But it wasn't an angel of light type scenario. Dennis saw himself as more of a vigilante.

He started to spend the night on the floor of her room. Rochelle was disturbed at first. She just wanted to be left alone so the quiet could eat her whole. But there was a comfort in hearing the same rhythmic breathing that used to send her off to sleep.

The kids at school were talking about Ricky. Ricky the junior who was always trying out for basketball but could never make the team.

"I get he was a loser but that's no reason for someone to beat the snot out of him," Belinda Devine said in the hall before third period. Rochelle thought she was going to be sick. Two weeks later she still had that feeling. And that's when she knew.

"Don't tell them, Ro. Just come with me. We can make it on our own. We have my car. I've been looking through the want ads. I can find something. I can take care of us." They were sitting in Dennis's basement which is what they called it now. Rochelle was wearing a powder blue sweatsuit and sat ankles crossed on Dennis's bed. They had burnt her miniskirts and hot pants in a barrel in the backyard. When their father asked what in the Sam Hill they were doing, Rochelle said, "Science class." He had gone back inside.

"They say Ricky almost died, Dennis." She didn't know why that bothered her. For what she went through, she figured his death would be a fair enough trade. But she couldn't stop rubbing her finger against that errant stitch.

"And? Some people deserve to hurt, Ro." He was sitting criss-cross applesauce with his notebook in his lap. There was something dark on the page he kept working at with his pen. "I don't make the rules." He sounded matter of fact about it like he had received word from upper management.

Looking at her brother, hunched over on concrete in a dingy white t-shirt, Rochelle finally put her finger on why it bothered her so much. It was because it didn't bother Dennis in the slightest.

• • • •

THEIR PARENTS DIDN'T put up a fight. Their mother was too tired, and their father didn't really care. Rochelle was kind of holding out on the certainty that her father would at least want her to get her diploma. But he just turned it into a positive. "Work will be good for you both."

She never said anything about the baby.

Dennis found them a cheap enough duplex. He found work as a night janitor at City Hall. He worked at the gas station during the day. Rochelle found a temp agency willing to hire her, and she prayed nightly to no one that she'd find a position where she didn't have to face the kids at school. Because when Ricky came back, he told everyone he hooked up with Rochelle and that her crazy brother jumped him. She couldn't tell them the truth because the truth was worse than the lie.

Their parents began to fade away. Without the kids in the house, they had to look each other in the eye and communicate. Instead of bringing them together, it had the opposite effect.

Bradford left one evening and never came back. Eileen stayed in the house. She found a job at the dry cleaner and called Rochelle sometimes to tell her how she liked having her freedom. But Bradford called from his new apartment in Missouri one evening. One of the checks he sometimes sent Eileen out of guilt or pity hadn't been cashed. He kept calling her about it, but she never picked up. He had their neighbor, Mrs. Poke check on her. When the police finally came to break down the door, they found Eileen dead in the tub and Dean Martin crooning from the record player.

"Dennis, what have we done?" Rochelle said sitting on their kitchen floor, the receiver still cradled between her neck and shoulder.

"Nothing," Dennis said, calmly scanning the water bill. "We don't make the rules."

Chapter Ten

She was afraid of Mack's face. Not the pain of childbirth. Not the horror of having it in the bathtub with Dennis as her midwife. Not the realization that her childhood would soon be deader than an unlucky cat.

She was afraid that all she would see was Ricky.

But Mack didn't look like Ricky. He didn't look much like Rochelle either. He was scrunched up with a black toupee of hair that tickled his forehead. He fit perfectly in her arms and took to her breast while Dennis had to discard the placenta. The bathroom was a bloody mess, but Dennis soon made it shine.

Rochelle looked into her son's face. There she saw her father leaving. Her mother dying at her own hand. She saw being on top of an unsteady world and then being pulled down into the wet grass. While Mack ate his breakfast, Rochelle wondered if she still had a soul. If she ever had one in the first place.

• • • •

DENNIS WAS UNMOVED by Mack. He never asked to hold him, but it didn't bother Rochelle. Dennis did all the cleaning and cooking. She wasn't going to nag him to hold her baby, too.

They found a nice lady that lived at their duplex. Ms. Mulligan was seventy-two and perhaps a bit too advanced in years to look after a newborn, but she was kind and agreed to lock up her cat whenever Mack was over. She also didn't charge anything.

Rochelle hated leaving him, but she loved it, too. She liked wearing pretty clothes and working with people she didn't have to change or burp. For a time she worked at the photo lab pretending she couldn't identify the people she knew on the film she developed. Sometimes, she thought bleach wouldn't be enough to burn the images away. She went on to work at the department store where she spritzed perfume in people's faces, and then it was the laundromat where her mother had worked and everyone noted the resemblance. She saw plenty of kids she used to go to school with, but it was never a problem. Nobody said a word to her.

And due to Ricky's ingenious idea to steal a cop car, she never saw him again. She figured this meant he was as good as dead, and that was the story she'd always stick with.

At night, she'd tuck Mack in and lay down next to him. His body was proof that good things came from the ugliest situations. But as she'd hold him and softly cry into his hair, ugly was the only thing Rochelle ever felt.

• • • •

"YOU NEED A GIRLFRIEND," Rochelle said as she picked at her tiny chicken breast and mashed potatoes. Dennis rolled his eyes.

"Why do you go and say stuff like that, Ro?" He was still wearing his janitor's uniform even though he had switched to the day shift and got off earlier than her now. They bumped his pay and promoted him to overseeing the entire cleaning staff, so sometimes they could afford meat.

"Stuff like what? A woman would be good for you."

Dennis grunted into his plate. "Good for me. Nobody knows what's good for me," he said. He was thinking about cats, about the one in Ms. Mulligan's duplex. His breathing started to slow.

"I don't mean it like that. I just mean, you need someone other than me to boss you around." She smiled but Dennis didn't.

"You don't boss me around, Ro."

"Oh you know what I mean. I'm always–"

"You don't boss me around, Ro!" Dennis's fist was rock against table. Mack started to scream.

Rochelle went and took Mack out of his bassinet and shushed him against her. She danced in a little circle hoping Dennis couldn't see how scared she was. But Dennis wasn't even paying attention to her. He was cerebrally mutilating everyone who had ever made him feel second hand.

"I-I'm sorry, Dennis," Rochelle whispered. Dennis finally saw her and blinked himself back to the present. He scratched at the back of his head. He stared at her, at Mack in her arms.

"I take care of us. Right, Ro?" Rochelle pressed her lips into each other. She nodded when she realized there was no other option.

• • • •

MS. MULLIGAN'S CAT suddenly went missing, so Rochelle sat with her awhile one day after work. She was overwhelmed by the love that was framed on Ms. Mulligan's walls and the piano pushed against the bay window in her living room.

"Your husband?" Rochelle asked. Ms. Mulligan was looking above the piano, out the window with a heart hoping Cheddar would soon come back.

"Oh, Louis. Yes, he is. Was. But is." She smiled at a joke she thought she told. Rochelle smiled, too.

"I hope to find love like that one day."

"It wasn't all sunshine and roses." Emotion was hitting her. Her hurt for Cheddar was replaced with that old tug that had dulled over the years. Matilda Mulligan closed her eyes. She spoke to me. "He used to gamble, and I was a horrible nag at times. But we found Christ. If it weren't for Him, well, he would have left." She heard the house settle and hope swirled in her chest again. "Or we would have killed each other."

Rochelle felt uncomfortable. She felt like there was somebody in the room she couldn't see. Her parents were church-raised and took them to Mass but neither really knew me. She had a friend, Margot, who was her science lab partner who talked to her about Jesus once, but Rochelle brushed her off. She kept looking at the door hoping Matilda would get the hint.

And Matilda did but didn't acknowledge it. "You don't know about Jesus, do you?"

"I know enough," Rochelle said. Something in her redirected her focus. She started listing in her head the things she had to do when she got back to the duplex. She willed Mack to start screaming.

"Nobody can ever know enough," Matilda said. She missed Louis, and that feeling sometimes tried to sit next to her. But whenever she'd close her eyes and talk to me, I'd fill the hole in her lonely heart. "I imagine you haven't lived this life sinless have you?" Her eyes were soft, a rheumy blue. Rochelle could tell from the photos that Matilda was pretty once. But how quickly pretty no longer mattered.

"I'm not a horrible person, if that's what you're asking."

"That's not what I'm asking." Matilda could feel it. Cheddar wasn't coming back. It was the same feeling when Louis went to work that morning all those years ago.

"I guess, I guess I've done things I shouldn't have." The faces flooded Rochelle. All the boys she let touch her.

"Welcome to being human, love." Matilda smiled. She remembered everything. Even the breakfast she had served. Two eggs over easy, peppered grits, cup of strong coffee. She didn't get to kiss Louis on the top of his head like she did every morning while he ate. She had to leave early to wash the Henderson's whites.

"Thing is, it never goes away, your debt. You rack up a lifetime of sin, of bad deeds, crooked thoughts, poor intentions. And you tell yourself you can nag it away. You can gamble it away. But there's not enough money in the world." Louis had worked at the pharmacy where he did odd jobs for Mr. Jacobs. He swept and mopped the floors. Wiped down the counters. Stocked the shelves. Mr. Jacobs was always praising Louis on his work ethic, which Matilda figured was quite generous for a white man. Sometimes, names were called. But Mr. Jacobs never let those kids sit at the counter waiting for their sodas. He did the good thing, the right thing and kicked them out of the pharmacy.

Rochelle stopped looking at the door. "Okay, but then what? Positive thinking? Spiritual enlightenment? I hear Hare Krishna is still all the rage." It came out viciously but only because Rochelle was scared. Cheddar was gone, and her brother was a lunatic. And she was a lunatic for living with him. But the deep down fear was the one Rochelle didn't handle and didn't weigh. Her good heart yearned for me, but her bad mind kept me away.

"He paid it all on the cross. He was crucified, died, and was buried, and on the third day, after defeating Satan in hell, He was resurrected. He died for you, Rochelle. Don't you know that?" It wasn't Matilda so much anymore. It was me, digging beneath skin and fat and into bone and through the hardened parts of Rochelle's chest. She gasped in breath as if she could feel her sternum cracking.

"He paid it all. And now we're free." Matilda got home around noon where a police officer met her at the front door. Louis had been walking from the bus stop to the pharmacy. Those same kids had skipped school to jump him. He hit his head against the curb and couldn't be revived. "Don't you want to be free, Rochelle?" Matilda said, closing her eyes again, reminding herself that she still was.

Rochelle felt her chest and breathed in deep. She looked at Mack balled up in the carrier at her feet. Freedom sounded nice, like a foreign country she'd heard of but never been to. But the reality was that nobody was free when choices linked together like a noose. Like Dennis, she didn't make the rules.

She grabbed the carrier and looked at Ms. Mulligan's warm brown face, her eyes blue with truth as she turned to leave. "I'm sorry about your cat." And Rochelle was. She was very sorry.

• • • •

MACK GREW OLDER AND Rochelle was at first reminded of a flower and then of a wayward weed. It was terrible to think about her son that way, but he wasn't like the other kids. He didn't want to learn his letters. He could barely count to ten. They were at the pediatrician once and a boy younger than him was listing all the presidents in order. Rochelle nearly burst a blood vessel.

"Why did you give me a dunce?" She viciously asked her pillow. She was ashamed a few seconds later when the only answer she got was the question echoing in her head.

"School will be great. You're going to love school. You're such smart boy." Rochelle pulled herself together. It was her first day at Augustus, Norton, and Davies and Mack's first day of kindergarten. The words were balled up in her throat. She had a hard time talking anymore. Her son was sitting at the breakfast table where she smeared too much jelly on his toast. She ignored a glob that fell on his shirt.

"It's scary." Mack had a hard time talking, too, but not for the same reasons.

"Scary? You're six! What do you have to be scared about?" Rochelle said to the can of Spaghetti O's in the cabinet. Everything made her sad, and there was a cloud of guilt where her demon swirled its sharp nail around her head.

Mack stared at the jelly on his shirt. He knew it was bad, the things Uncle Dennis did. The things Uncle Dennis showed him. But he stayed quiet. He refused to hurt his mother that way.

When he didn't speak she whirled at him, anger now pounding in her chest. "Come on, Mack. You can put more than two words together. It's not going to kill you," she said, having words with the pillow in her head.

• • • •

SHE KNEW GLENN AUGUSTUS liked her. She played carefully with that interest because if she was smart, she could fill in permanently for the last secretary who went AWOL. It wasn't hard, catering to a man. She already instinctively knew what he wanted.

"Rochelle, you're a genius," he said when he tasted the fresh cup of coffee she brought him. The other partners nodded curtly at her when she came in that morning, taking a generous glance at her backside when she turned to leave, but Glenn was personable. He had no qualms about making his affections known although he was still technically married.

"Oh, it can't be that great," she smiled, sipping from her own cup. She left a dark red lip stain on the rim.

"Sit," he said. And she did. She noticed he went to close the door. "I know this is your first day and all, but we have a real need for someone like you." She got the feeling the "we" wasn't necessary. "Eleanor, my old secretary, isn't coming back. Her mother has dementia." Glenn looked down at his cup, and Rochelle tried to ignore the faded white ring around his left ring finger. "I want you, Rochelle," he said, and when he looked into her eyes, he erased her history.

"Absolutely," she said and laughed as I watched the demon whisper in her ear.

· · · ·

EACH DAY WAS A HARDENED tumor in Rochelle's gut. Mack was no longer the small, malleable boy she could win back over with a side hug or an off-centered kiss.

He hated her now.

And he definitely hated Glenn Augustus.

She tried to rework and rebuild her life with a menagerie of self-help books. Little animals that opened their mouths and mewled at her, waiting to be opened and petted. Some of them weren't asinine. Some of them drew from biblical principles but none of them mentioned my name.

The blind leading the blind.

One day he came home and looked like death. He was wearing all black like usual, but his hand was bandaged, and he held it to his chest like a baby bird.

"What happened?" Her fear of him was extinguished by her motherly instinct. When he had left that morning, he had seemed normal. Relatively. But there was now a new layer of darkness that flapped at her like bird wings.

"Why do you care? Why are you even here?" Oddly enough, she took it as a good sign. He hardly ever spoke two words to her, his ears always hidden in his massive headphones.

She didn't tell him the real reason she'd come home early from her second aerobics class. That she was going to shower and change and head out with Glenn who had locked down tickets to the opera in Dallas. She pretended she was a good mother for once, and it was like edging bare feet against glass.

"Mack, I love you. I care about you. What happened?"

He laughed at her but his eyes looked like they'd been crying. When he sat, he shoved his head down, and she studied the hair she didn't get to see anymore. He was so much taller than her. And she knew he was at the point where she should be able to say "He's going to be a fine man one day." But also knew she couldn't.

"You only care about yourself," he said.

She quickly scanned the menagerie in her head but couldn't find the right page to tell her what to do. I breathed at her right shoulder, and she saw Ms. Mulligan in her head, the woman dead and gone. The woman who had a heart full of joy even when waist-deep in her own pain.

"I do all of this for us...for you." The lie is awkward, even for her. She did all of this for Glenn Augustus. Glenn who wanted her pretty and taut and didn't mind that she had a kid as long as he never had to see him. But she wouldn't let her mind go down that road. *I do it for Mack*, she thought, taking deliberate authority over her thoughts like it told her to in *You Can Heal Your Life*. She was doing it so her son could have a better existence which was an easy notion to get used to. Rochelle simply ignored the fact that her son already had one foot out the door.

"I'm going to my room," he said, benevolently giving her an out. All she could think about was holding his body against hers like she did when he was a baby.

But even Rochelle, who hoarded useless knowledge like pigs in a barn, knew it was too late for something like that.

Chapter Eleven

"**A**re you having the nightmares again?" Rochelle can't see Dr. Neese but she already knows the woman's mouth is twisted and puckered. Dr. Neese is by no means pretty. She's frazzled, that's the word Rochelle would use for her which is almost generous today. Dr. Neese's right hand shakes with caffeine tremors and her short curly hair is raising anarchy on her head. She's a woman who has a lot going for her: a lot of people, a lot of knowledge. But Dr. Neese has little to no self-regulation.

Rochelle knows this, but she doesn't stop seeing her because old habits die hard. Especially when you never try to break them.

"Yes. Always." There was one last night. They were at the kitchen table again. Dennis had just raised his voice at her, but this time he had Mack in his arms. His hand started to wrap around her son's small throat, and when she woke up, her own throat was screaming in the dark.

"He hurts him."

"It's only a dream," Dr. Neese says, chewing an aggressive divot into her pen. What Rochelle can't tell Dr. Neese is that it isn't just a dream. That it's truth. And that she knows this because I've revealed it to her.

"Maybe." Rochelle is self-conscious acting like a rag doll on a couch during the middle of the day. She knows Dr. Neese doesn't care. If the woman did, she wouldn't make her patients lie down like they've entered Freud's lair. But Rochelle is intimately tuned into the way her breasts lay pancake flat against her chest. The wide spread of her hips against the cushions. She isn't who she used to be. That's something we both agree on. But instead of looking into the renewed warmth in her heart, she keeps her wayward thoughts on the lie in the mirror.

"I know, Rochelle, that you're in your...group," Dr. Neese says, waving her pen in front of her in tic-toc swipes. "But maybe you need to be a part of something a little more...constructive." Rochelle smiles at the ceiling. She knows when Dr. Neese goes home, she'll put on sweatpants like the rest of the world and go looking for her cat under her bed. She'll stalk the Internet, hunting down her ex-boyfriend's new fiancée. She'll take inventory of all the things that make her better than this woman she's never met before in her life. She'll hold onto them like the still wet pen she clutches in her hand.

"It's constructive. They really care." Rochelle winces. She knows she sounds like a doddering fool. She's only ten years Dr. Neese's senior but she feels old and slow and like all the people she never wanted to be. But she isn't wrong. Her group at church, they love her. They're all action and don't stare at the clock like Dr. Neese. They want to know her, free of charge.

"I'm sure they do in their own little way. But I'm thinking we get you involved in something different. I know of a great therapy group that gets together for yoga and coffee. Just a group of chill women who don't want anything from you. They don't want to change you, Rochelle. They'll accept you for who you are." Rochelle smirks her response at the tiled ceiling above her. That's what a lot of people don't like about her now. The fact that she's changed.

Because it reminds them that change is something they might need to give a go someday too.

Rochelle gives herself a second to gather her sagginess and stretchiness. She collects herself and mentally tries to pull herself out of her body and into the moment. She looks Dr. Neese in the eye which is hard for her. And she can tell it's difficult for Dr. Neese, too.

"This hasn't been helping me. I appreciate you listening to me for all these years. But I always feel...lacking when I leave here. I don't mean that to be in any way offensive," Rochelle says. But then I take over. "You are so intelligent, Dr. Neese. Please never let that render you stupid." Dr. Neese looks bewildered and Rochelle's heart takes flight.

Her chains loosen around her neck.

• • • •

SHE KNOWS WHAT DENNIS did to Mack.

She just leaves it vague and void of detail which she imagines makes it even worse.

She didn't know back then. That's what she tells herself. Reassures herself with. But didn't she eventually catch on just a little bit? Like the time she and Mack played Scrabble and he started to cry quietly like he was sharing a moment with himself. Or that other time when she was off one rare Saturday and took him to the park. She tried to get him to play with the other kids, but he wouldn't move off the bench. He just sat and held her hand and studied the world working life out in front of him.

She should have hugged him more. That she regrets.

Rochelle cries so hard in her Jaguar, she stains the leather steering wheel. There's something else branching through her that she's tried to uproot the past several weeks.

Cancer. A tiny lump in her right breast. Stage three. A sliver of hope so small she keeps dropping it.

She doesn't know how to tell Glenn.

The dark thoughts braid and weave behind her eyes. They've been blinding her more and more. She tells the group about them and the group hears her out. They hold her hands and pray hard for her. But they've known me for so long that thoughts like this have never edged their way in.

Or so they say.

"Can you hear me?" she asks me, and I nod. There's a demon on the dashboard. He gnashes his teeth at me. I gently flick a finger at him, and he stalks closer to the windshield. "I feel...I feel so alone, Jesus. Nobody understands what this feels like. They're tired of me talking about it. I'm tired of me talking about it." Rochelle gulps in tears and air. She blasts the air conditioning at her face. "I feel so alone." I take her hand and hold it. She bends her head toward her lap. She doesn't say anything else, but no matter. I know her heart. She feels she's failed.

She feels she's doing this wrong. She's gotten baptized. She's accepted me.

But she feels no better.

I tell her it's all about her mind. It's all about what she's letting tip toe inside of it. I tell her it's all about guarding her heart. I tell her it's all about purpose.

Rochelle snorts and sends the demon skittering across the dash. "What purpose?" she asks.

And then her car phone begins to ring.

Chapter Twelve

"What do you like, Wrennie?" Wren looked up at her father, another question she wasn't expecting. He was always doing things like that. Digging through and looking under her rocks, trying to find what lay hidden there.

"I like purple, and I like the sun, and I like my tree, and I like Mommy..." Wren looks out the window because she can never stare directly at Mack's face. "And I like you."

She looks over, makes sure his eyes are back on the road. She watches his lips lift into a smile, and she looks at his hand clutching the steering wheel, the one with the black tattoo. It's a heart but not a pretty heart. It's the organ that beats inside her chest like Daddy told her. Sometimes, when they're out looking for car parts, ladies like to stare at his hand and then roll their eyes up to the clouds. And Wren feels such pain that it borders on hatred. Because she knows those same ladies pick their noses and scratch their behinds and yell at their perfectly good husbands.

It's another one of her rocks. The one that protects the truth.

"I like you, too, Wrennie," Daddy says before turning up their music, their music that's loud and angry and never really has much to say. Sometimes Daddy turns it off, his face far off and no longer in the truck. Sometimes he turns it up and drums his fingers on the steering wheel while Wren makes up words to the songs.

She looks over again at his heart-marked hand and the fingers that tap against the wheel. She hovers her own hand out in the chasm between them.

••••

SHE'S SEEN THEM BEFORE when they're on the bed or on the couch, her mother a seashell inside of her father. They cry and it's loud in her ears even though it's really very soft. She doesn't like seeing Daddy cry. She's okay when Mommy cries. There's something more natural about it.

She always gets the urge to go up and crawl in between the both of them. To take their hands and hold them to her heart. But there's something so deeply connected when they softly shake into their pain that Wren feels like she's outside of the house, looking through the window.

And besides, she knows there's nothing she can really do.

She's only a little girl.

• • • •

SOMETIMES SHE STAYS with Mimi when Mommy and Daddy work. Once she stayed with Abuelo. Mommy wants her to do preschool but Daddy says school is for losers. Mommy hits him on the arm.

She likes Mimi's house. It's very big, and there's a large pool in the back. Grandpa Glenn uses a long handled net to scoop up leaves. He taught her how to do this once then went back inside to make a few phone calls.

When Mimi found her by herself with the skimmer, she wasn't very happy.

But mostly, time with Mimi is some of her favorite time. Mimi likes to bake cookies with her and took her out to ride a horse once. Sometimes they go to the park or get ice cream.

One time, she told Daddy that Mimi must have been the best mom, besides Mommy of course. He didn't say anything, just turned up the music.

• • • •

THERE'S A MAN IN THE wedding photo that Daddy and Mommy won't talk about. He has dark hair like Daddy's and stands next to Mimi in the photo. There's something about him that Wren tries to dissect.

"Who's this?" she asked one time with the frame tucked in her arm like a baby. Her mother was taking a bath and Daddy was sitting and waiting to leave like he does some nights though he won't ever tell her where he goes.

"Mr. Regret."

"He live near us?"

"Yes. Unfortunately."

"Do I know him?"

"No, fortunately," Daddy said. The light in the living room half-shadowed Mommy who was now standing damp in the doorway.

"What you got, baby girl?" she asked. She was wearing her blue terry cloth robe and naked feet.

"Mr. Regret," Wren said, and Daddy laughed loudly in her ear.

• • • •

SHE DOESN'T REMEMBER the last day. It hurts when she tries to construct it in her mind. She knows there was ice cream and their music crammed tight between them in the truck cab and Roy McGruffin that became hers when moments before he hadn't even existed.

But she only knows that last part because Mommy told her.

What she does remember is the night.

She woke up to find Mommy alone in her bed and Daddy alone in a tree. And even though she stood close to him hovering above her and then stood close to Mommy who stayed belly flat against their porch's wooden floor, the one thing that bites at her like acid on her skin is the fact that she was there. With each of them.

And neither one even noticed.

• • • •

AT THE FUNERAL, HER skin itched. She didn't scratch at it and didn't tell anyone, not even Mimi who asked her every ten seconds if she was okay.

It didn't seem like a good time to talk to Mommy about anything.

The itching began to burn when Grandpa Glenn held her waist, and she hovered above Daddy who wasn't Daddy. She felt like the lead character in a play, like everyone was expecting something from her, so she dipped down and kissed his cheek that tasted like Mommy's make up.

After the funeral she kept her mind off the itching, the burning, the chemical taste of her father in her mouth by dry swallowing carrot sticks and explaining to her baby cousin, Antonio, how Daddy had died.

Wren likes to think Antonio would have clapped if his arms had been strong enough.

That night, Mommy wants her to sleep with her. And Wren tells her yes even though she wants to be alone in her bed and cry into Roy's chewed up fur. Instead, she lets Mommy hold her, and Wren smashes her face into her pillow.

She won't cry. She has to be strong for Mommy.

• • • •

"WHAT WE NEED IS AN adventure." Even at four, it sounds like a distraction. But Wren makes her face happy, working her arm fat with her pinching fingers where Mommy can't see. She has Roy on her lap and places her chin on top of his worn, fuzzy head.

"Where are we going?"

"A new exciting place called Arkansas."

"Mimi and Grandpa Glenn coming?"

"No, sweetie."

Wren bit her lip. It would be hard to shoulder the burden all alone, but maybe she could use her happy voice for a couple of days to keep Mommy focused.

"Okay," she says and breaks out into a big smile.

"Wren, we're going to be so happy living there," Mommy says. Her long black hair frames her face like curtains.

"I know," Wren says weakly. She grabs her mother's hand with its missing tattoo.

• • • •

MIMI CRIES A LOT. HER face is red and puffy, and she takes her magic pills Dr. Nease prescribed her. She's mad–"but not at you, little duck"–and then her eyes narrow like she's staring someone down.

Grandpa Glenn doesn't seem to be too fazed.

That's the last time she sees Mimi before they leave. Mama explains they have to hurry because she has a job waiting for her. And Wren imagines the job is dressed all nice in a suit and tie, waiting expectantly at a restaurant while he asks the waiter for more bread.

The move is an adventure but not the best kind. She's stuck in the back of the car with Roy McGruffin, and she falls asleep to Mommy singing about it being too late with Carole King.

When she wakes up, they're there. Wherever there is.

• • • •

SHE GOES TO A PLACE called Little Chicks. There are no chicks there to pet. Just screaming children and women who carry heavy weight in their arms and legs. They're nothing like Mommy who's thin and beautiful and everything Wren will want to be when she grows up. Except for Ms. Melanie, but she has a mean face.

Wren doesn't like the way the women look at Mommy when she turns her back to leave.

It's not horrible until Father's Day rolls around. They make key chains but Wren cuts a long line of rawhide and beads it like a bracelet. "For Daddy," she says to Jamie Hooper who has a finger up his nose. *For Daddy,* she says, but this time inside her head.

• • • •

FOR HER FIFTH BIRTHDAY, they go to Dairy Queen. Mommy gets ice cream dipped in chocolate, and Wren gets a cup of vanilla with M&Ms sprinkled on top. She watches Mommy bite into the chocolate and then lick the vanilla underneath. She's methodical about it like she's here, but she's not really here.

"How old was Daddy?" Wren asks her ice cream.

Mommy shoves the palm of her hand into one eye but then returns to her work. She tastes the vanilla on her lips when she says, "Twenty-six."

"How old are you?" Wren asks.

"Twenty-seven."

"What does being grown up feel like?" A small family—a mother, father, and little boy—sits down at the bench next to them.

Mommy looks like she's thinking hard on this one. She looks at the family and then looks at Wren. "It feels like making all the decisions and having nobody to blame but yourself."

That night, Mommy has her tummy troubles. Sometimes, Wren can hear it in the background of her conscience, her mother making friends with the toilet. She usually cries afterwards, and Wren drifts off to the sound of Mommy's head making contact with the bathroom wall. But this time there's no crying or soft thud of skull against plaster. So Wren tiptoes to their shared bathroom where Mommy lays on the ground, Wren takes the dirty washcloth from the edge of the tub and stands on her plastic stool in front of the sink. She lets cool water soak it through before she wrings it hard and wipes down Mommy's sweaty face. Mommy looks up at her, and when she realizes what she's doing, her eyes look like two birds frantic in their cages. But Wren puts her hand on Mommy's cheek and smiles into those eyes.

Because Wren knows blaming herself is a battle her mother will never win.

• • • •

SHE DOESN'T LIKE RHONDA very much. Actually, she doesn't mind Rhonda as much as she minds Rhonda's mother.

The woman is loud and invades the apartment like she owns it. Her feet on the coffee table, screaming pink nail polish on her toes. To Wren, they look like tiny pigs waving flags.

Rhonda's mother holds her own mother hostage while Wren pretends to sleep or stealthily eyes them from the hallway. I stand next to Wren while she watches. While her heart pounds her ribs.

"Remember, not everyone makes a good friend," her mother sometimes says when Wren gets home tired from the politics of Little Chicks.

Wren watches Rhonda's mother fill up her glass with liquid from the brown bottle on the coffee table. She takes the glass and tilts her head back, shiny teeth bared to the ceiling.

• • • •

FOR A WHILE THINGS are quiet.

And then they're not.

She's sitting at the toy bin with Connor and his sister Misti. Connor has a bowl cut and a crusty red scab below his left eye and his sister doesn't seem to fare any better with the palm-sized bruise on her bicep. Wren had felt a tug of empathy the first time she saw their tiny bodies marked up that way, the abrasions landing in different places depending on what day it was. But then Connor had to go and open his mouth.

"You're such a doo-doo faced bird brain." Connor is grabbing up tiny plastic soldiers with a sticky hand and doesn't even have the decency to look Wren in the eye when he says it. Misti laughs, her unwashed hair too close to Wren's nose.

Maybe he's right, she thinks, and before I can touch the top of her head, the one with the coffee-colored strands growing closer to her shoulders, she's cohabited with the thought and made a nice bed for it.

"Wren." Ms. Melanie is in the doorway. Her face looks unlike the face she always gives. The meanness is gone. Wren is worried.

Behind Ms. Melanie are two police officers. Wren takes a trip back to her tree and remembers the breeze on her face and her father's feet as the police cars rolled up into their yard. There was one, a young black man who was new to the force who put a blanket on her shoulders and sat with her inside the house. She remembered he was kind enough. Kind enough when everybody else had forgotten to be.

"Uh-oh! Doodie Police are here!" Connor says, and the last thing Wren will ever remember from her old life is the sound of Misti laughing.

Chapter Thirteen

Rochelle's body is an angry road map. The inflammation swells behind tissue, twists and turns within the fibrous lining of her breasts. She imagines them gone. She sees herself looking at where they used to live in a long piece of glass and places her dream hands on her bony cage. She moves them over the hardened surface; the only soft thing existing anymore, the heart that lies beneath it.

But even that is starting to stiffen a bit.

She wakes on the plane. The air is stale and the club soda she asked for, rotting in her mouth. She really wants ginger ale, but she can imagine the drink accelerating the cancerous lump, prodding it along with sugary fingers. Besides, she already has a headache.

The excitement has worn off. She wants to see Wren so much, she's started to ache in her joints. But when the social worker called that morning, she casually mentioned how Rochelle would be responsible for taking Wren to see Natalie on a weekly basis. "Once Dr. Carol gives consent, of course," was the nasally whistle in Rochelle's ear. Dr. Carol. Rochelle had to work her lip with her teeth partly to keep from laughing and partly from throwing up.

Now it's trash thrown away, seatbacks in the upright position, and tray tables locked in place. It's the strained sound of an ancient plane descending, the wind battering at it, but the plane doesn't think to turn back like a sane, sentient being. Instead it propels forward, slightly taking a dive into the unknown until the wheels delicately kiss solid ground.

• • • •

WREN CAN'T SIT STILL and neither can Roy. They travel from the couch where her mother isn't, to her bedroom where her mother isn't, to the kitchen where only an accordion partition in the window

84

separates her from the social worker. Denise. She's outlined in black. Black mascara, and black tight curls, and a black dress over black tights, and black heeled boots. She smiles, her lips thankfully untouched by the darkness, but there's a slightly forced tone to the way she talks, like she's counting down the minutes in the back of her head.

Today, Mimi comes. It's why Wren got to come home to the apartment. She had been staying with a foster family, the Mastersons, a couple who couldn't have children and tried to turn all three of them into blood relatives. *You can't turn cough syrup into blood,* she had said in her head where Roy read her thoughts. *No-siree-bob. But maybe we still be nice to them. Maybe it's hard not having what you want.* And Wren nodded with his fur tucked under her chin, trying not to cry.

The last few days were fastened securely behind her, which means she can breathe a little bit easier now. But when she does, she can only smell the faint traces of her mother who is nowhere to be found.

· · · ·

SHE WAS LUCKY. AND she knew that. One year of rehab and psychiatric evaluation. The guy in the Bronco lived. Her heart almost took a stroll right out of her mouth when she heard that. First time drug offense, a miniscule amount of coke. The single mother card was played, no priors.

She wanted to blame it all on Mary, make her take the stand. But deep down, she knew Mary was right. She was nothing but a bulldozer.

"We should be throwing a party," her attorney (courtesy of Glenn) had said, a fierce looking redhead who threw caution to the wind when choosing her pink power suit that morning.

"Break out the noise makers," Natalie said.

Her room—no, the room she's staying in, she reminds herself—is the dullest shade of taupe to keep her from getting over-excited. Or over-angry. Or over-anything.

The first week, her eye still stung from the altercation in the cell where they were holding her before trial. A prostitute had landed her fist into the right side of Natalie's face for sitting on the wrong bench. The sting was like an electrical current that snapped something inside of her brain. She looked at the woman like prey that needed to be hunted. And then she offered her own fist.

She thought that would have affected the case, but apparently the guard on duty was too lazy to mention it. Her lawyer ignored the green blob on her cheek, and the defense attorney seemed too enthralled by the pink power suit to take note.

What a lucky duck I am, Natalie thought, trying hard to ignore the strong smell of newly mopped floors. Now at The Peaceful Palms—a rehab facility forty miles north of White Smoke— Natalie sits in a room the color of putty and a small whisper in the back of her brain wants to confront the truth, sift through her past.

"No," Natalie says out loud to no one. Because she's spent too much time trying to make things make sense.

Maybe it's the taupe.

• • • •

"YOU CAN'T LEAVE." IT'S the thing Dr. Cohen had said when she told him about Natalie. "You need treatment."

Rochelle knew he was right. But she also knew the opportunity God was giving her, and if she traded it for surgery and chemo, she'd have to watch any chance of reconnecting with her granddaughter fade away. Besides, she was pretty sure her stubbornness alone would keep her heart pumping.

Five months in, she's almost ready to reconsider that decision. Wren is in the kitchen playing with the play dough they made with flour and salt. They colored it with red food dye, so both of them look like they've recently committed a heinous crime. Rochelle places one of her hands between the breasts she still has. She feels for her heart. She looks at the cordless on Natalie's bedside table. She calls Glenn.

"Hello." He says it like he's the one who's calling. She puts on each syllable like a coat and hat. The relief is instantaneous.

"I just needed to hear you say that," she breathes.

"What's troubling you?" Glenn breathes back. He's lying on the bed they share together with a young woman who looks slightly like his wife. She's no more than twenty and crinkles her eyes at him when she smiles.

"I...you know, nothing. Nothing, Glenn. Just miss you is all." Rochelle plants her red-stained hand harder against the truth. She wants to ask him to visit, monthly maybe, because a year is too long without him. She's not allowed to leave the state with Wren.

But there's something etched between them as delicate as lace. Rochelle can feel it's webbing dividing them, holding back everything she needs to say. She knows her friend, Ann, will ask if Glenn came to see her, and she'll have to brush her off with a "work" excuse. But she knows this has nothing to do with Glenn's work and everything to do with the world he's created. Her being in White Smoke right now has nothing to do with that world.

"Miss you, too," Glenn says, planting his lips against somebody else's hair.

• • • •

THEY SAY ALL KINDS of things at school. She almost wishes she had someone to talk to. Maybe even Rhonda but Rhonda goes to the school on the other side of town.

That's okay, you know. We've got Mimi. And the people at church seem nice. Wren knows Roy's just being empathetic. Mimi is nice to have, but she isn't Mommy. And people at church are old and some of them smell kind of funny.

What about the dresses? You look very pretty in them. And Jesus sounds like He's a good man. Yes, that's true.

"He's also God," Wren says because she learned that one the hard way. She had said the same thing to a group of women clucking like hens around Mimi, that Jesus was a nice man. And one of the smelly ones shot back: *He's God, you know.*

Roy did the impression for weeks, placing his paw near his collar like he was the Queen of Sheba.

They both lie on Wren's bed, choking on a fit of giggles.

"I have you, too," she whispers in Roy's ear, and then they both close their eyes to sleep.

• • • •

THEY'VE HAD SEVERAL visits at this point–twenty-nine to be exact–and on each one, Rochelle has looked like death. Natalie has had enough decency not to mention it, although today, the vegetables tasted raw at lunch, and Dr. Carol wouldn't let up on Natalie's "feelings of victimization." So she decides to let off a little steam.

"Rochelle, you look like a dump truck's rolled over you. What gives?" She watches Rochelle shift on the white leather couch, the noise an unlady-like contrast to the baby blue sweater set she's wearing. It's early March, and it's a hot one in White Smoke. But Rochelle doesn't look like she'll give way to short sleeves any time soon.

"Wren, baby. Do you mind if Mimi has a minute alone?" Natalie's eyes roll hard in their sockets. She's been noticing little bits of Camp Rochelle staking claim on her territory. The way she always has a hand on Wren's back. The cutesy voice she uses to control the conversation. The countless times she refers to how tired Natalie seems and that maybe she'll want Rochelle to stick around when her time at rehab is up next month.

Fat chance, Natalie thinks.

When Wren moves to the table and chairs in the middle of the room, Rochelle picks tiny blue threads from her sweater. "Cancer," she says.

It socks the breath out of Natalie's lungs. She's sad, and angry, and hateful all in one swift move. She pushes her heels down into the cheap tile floor to keep from flinging her feet at Rochelle's face. How could she do this? How could she do this to Wren?

How can she do this to me? Natalie thinks before quickly releasing the thought.

"I should have told you."

"You think so, do you? So what's going to happen? You croak, and I'm stuck here, and Wren gets thrown back into foster care?"

"It's not that bad," Rochelle lies.

"Then I'd hate to see bad." Natalie is crying, which makes her even angrier. She gets up gingerly, trying to keep the tasteless couch quiet and goes to hug her daughter. She places her face at the top of Wren's head, Wren who's hugging hard on Roy McGruffin's neck. But Wren keeps her body stiff, and Natalie pretends she doesn't notice.

• • • •

IT FLEW, THE TIME. Wren is brushed, and polished, and beautiful in a new dress Rochelle bought for her, and looking at her hurts.

"Time to go, little duck." The social worker is waiting outside at the apartment. She suggested taking Wren alone to "ease the transition." So these are the last moments Rochelle has Wren all to herself. At least she has comfort knowing she's been baptized.

"Who loves you?" Rochelle asks.

"Mimi."

"And?"

"Mommy."

"And?"

"Jesus." Rochelle nods and holds her tight. She holds onto the truth even as her mind carefully sifts for thoughts of Glenn like a fishing net.

• • • •

ROCHELLE IS GONE AND Natalie breathes relief. But she's also heartbroken. She thought she'd get to say one last goodbye to the closest thing to a mother she's had in a long time. But that would be painting a rosy picture. That wouldn't be telling the truth.

Instead, she's greeted by the social worker, and Wren who hides behind her stuffed dog shyly. She goes and gives Wren a hug, but all she feels is the lumpy softness of her husband's past.

"We've got a big job to do, baby girl." And it was one. In the next few days, Natalie gathers her letters of recommendation from Dr. Carol and a few other staff at The Peaceful Palms. She dresses up her resume, opting to glaze over her year-long hiatus, and takes Wren to the library so they can print it out. She becomes increasingly concerned as Wren stays quiet and looks at her with her bare brown eyes, searching Natalie's face for answers. And Natalie becomes increasingly annoyed when Wren shoves off into her room and talks to that stuffed dog for hours.

The phone rings a few times one of the days Natalie is craving a pint of vodka. She lets the recorder pick up and then deletes the message when she hears Rochelle's voice.

Finally, the big day comes. Natalie wears one of the pantsuits Women Who Work gave her. She feels obnoxiously like her redheaded lawyer. They drive to JCC, and Natalie swallows down the bile swiftly rising in her throat. She doesn't want to face Tara McMahon who could rip her in two even with a pity sneer. She doesn't want to see the faces of her former team as she walks the long, empty space between their cubicles and Tara's office. She doesn't want one of those faces to be Mary's that she might just claw off in the alley behind the building.

She doesn't want any of it. But then she looks down at Wren who's absorbing her through her pupils.

"You need to stay here, baby girl. I've got to go inside and hopefully change our lives." She feels terrible Wren has to sit alone in the parking lot, but she doesn't have any other options. She's fortunate enough that Glenn agreed to pay her lawyer fees, not to mention her rent that he's still paying until she can get back on her feet. She doesn't like the pity pay-off or the weight of having to do something monumental just to get things back to normal, especially when normal wasn't that stellar to begin with.

She doesn't like that she can't even afford a babysitter for her daughter. And she most certainly doesn't like the way that stuffed dog is looking at her.

But she goes inside. It's a risky move so close to lunch but Tara's car is still there. She spends ten minutes convincing Susan, the secretary–a loud mouth older lady who treats everyone like her small-minded child–that she needs to see Tara immediately, and finally, she gets a little face time. But that time is short-lived and clouded by Mary who darts her eyes at Natalie like two very sharp knives.

In the car, she knows her face is bloated by the tears she's cried in the parking lot. She avoids Wren's face when she gets inside.

"New plan. From now on, we don't rely on anyone to throw us a bone. We take what we want, what we need. Because nobody is going to do it for us," she says, and Wren's raw eyes barely understand when Natalie takes Roy and sends him sailing to the back of the car.

• • • •

NATALIE WON'T ANSWER her calls. This terrifies her but also gives her a sick sense of closure. It's confirmation that Rochelle isn't crazy and that her daughter-in-law needs help. But it's also confirmation that Rochelle won't be the one giving it.

When she got home, Glenn wasn't around. She thought maybe he'd pick her up from the airport, but she only got the machine when she called after landing. So she took a taxi back home and found a quickly scribbled note about a tennis game. In an instant, she saw a woman behind her closed lids and thought she could smell the cloying scent of overripe perfume. But she shook it off. Her mind and body couldn't take that sort of suspicion.

She went to her bedroom, pawed through the luggage she struggled upstairs, and that, too, was too much to bear. She found her Bible lying on top of her clothes. She held it next to her on the bed, hugged it like the person that wasn't there and let her head rest on the pillow.

"Help," was the single-worded prayer Rochelle whispered until it lost all meaning.

• • • •
Now

Chapter Fourteen
Wren

I rip my shirt from my cracked laundry basket and assault my nose with it. It smells like yesterday and all the yesterdays before that one. Smoke, grime, the ever lurking threat of Principal Zinberg.

But most of all Marek.

"Mmm...regret," I mutter in a half-sleep haze. I soak the shirt in wet puffs of the cotton candy body spray Mareck swiped from the Piggly Wiggly. When I'm done, I don't dare take another whiff. Just put it on and try to avoid the way it feels like a crusted diaper on my skin.

What is, is, as Jerr-Bear always says.

I leave my room after fishing out my Catholic school girl skirt I got at Goodwill and head to our tuna can of a bathroom, a small sliver of room where I take record showers and glare at my face in a mirror that I'm not entirely sure is made out of glass. It has an accordian door, a rather ludicrous choice for a bathroom. And no matter how hard I try to get it to click against the jamb, it always pops open just enough to be indecent.

We have one rule in the apartment: keep all eyes off the bathroom door.

I put on the faucet and splash at my worn out face. I bite my tongue and attack my dry hair with a brush because I ran out of the detangling spray Mareck five-fingered at the big Wal-Mart in Junction. Make up takes roughly five seconds now because I have it down to a science: kohl-lined eyes, mascara, rouge on the cheeks, glittery lipgloss. With my Insane Clown Posse tee, I achieve the look that makes most mothers look twice.

My own, however, has bigger fish to fry.

"Hiya in there! Don't want to be late for my 6 AM with Mr. Porcelain," Jerry says, keeping to his own morning routine. He stays true to the bathroom rule and glues his face to the wood-paneled hallway wall with a newspaper in his hand. His back is doughy in his wife beater and his hairline could use a good trim, but I regrettably love him because I feel sorry for him, just like Mom does.

"All yours, Jerr-Bear." I slide past him, and my cheek practically scrapes the hung pictures on the wall. The "befores" as I like to think of them. Before Jerry. Before the ICP t-shirts. Before my father closed his eyes for good.

I swipe a pudding cup from the fridge for breakfast and lick the lid. The formica bites my back as I watch Mom shuffle her bunny slippers into the kitchen.

"Good morning."

"That's the rumor."

"Early shift today?"

"Yep. Greasy bacon and wandering hands. Friday's special." Mom sticks her head into the refrigerator in a way that reminds me of my favorite poet. Plath had gone and stuck her head in an oven instead. Much more effective and far less chilly if you ask me.

"Wren, think you might be late," Jerry says, his bathroom meeting now adjourned. He's dressed to repair air conditioning units, so he kind of comes off like a 1950's milkman.

"Jerr, you gotta make that green looking all spiffy like that? Dang, son. Be sure the ladies aren't home alone if you know what I mean." I elbow him into his pillowy side, and Jerr lets out a burnt-cheeked giggle.

"Oh, Wrennifer," he shakes his head. He grabs his lunchbox and kisses Mom's cheek at the refrigerator. I imagine it must feel like ice.

"Sleep well, my queen?" he asks Mom as he starts packing his powdered donuts. I look back at my pudding cup because looking at Jerry's hope makes me sad. I know what my mother really thinks. Sure, Jerry does well and was nice enough to let us move in after getting evicted from our trailer at Sunrise Estates. But he's no Brad Pitt and treats her a little too well. Not exactly my mother's type. I swallow down another glob of chocolate and the fear that always sits criss-cross applesauce in my throat.

"Can't sleep with you always on my mind," Mom says and grabs him. She gives him a real kiss this time that's likely to set Jerry's whole face on fire. Good, I think. Another day.

Because Natalie Reynolds is a lot of things, but she certainly isn't stupid. When Jerry had reluctantly come to Double Dee's with a few of his heating and cooling buddies, Mom had zoned in on him like a black widow. One guy was ruthlessly trying to get her number, but she shocked them all when she nodded at Jerry and said, "Who says good guys finish last?" He pocketed her digits like the golden ticket and returned for her at the end of her shift in his bright orange mini-van with the abrasively smiling A/C guy plastered on the side.

The rest, as the saying goes, is history.

"I hate to break up the family reunion, but I got a life to live, homeslices." I pop my pudding cup in the trash and salute with two slightly sticky fingers.

"Wren, come home. After school. I want to talk to you." The fear uncrosses its legs and sticks its feet into the sides of my throat. Moving. Again. I can read it in the thirty-seven years that have set up shop on my mother's face. Maybe I was wrong about the whole "not being stupid" thing.

"Yeah. Yeah, sure." I air kiss at Mom and Jerry and grab my bag. I make a quick run to my room and grab for a small bottle of glue underneath my mattress. I take a quick sniff, let the feeling of weightlessness run through me, then cram the glass bottle into my knock-off Timberlands.

As I put on my coat to keep January as far from me as humanly possible, I think about my name, the way it sounds when it comes out of people's mouths. The meaning: "a small songbird," the reason Mom chose it.

Most likely, the reason I'm trapped.

Outside my legs sting with cold, but I fight through the urge to go put on some tights. I'm not going to be like all those other suckers, slave to expectations regardless of how un-hypothermic their extremities might currently be.

I warm them up by running down the apartment staircase, past the Flores' apartment and its belly stabbing smell of eggs and fried meat, to where the frozen grass edges the parking lot. I see a wobbling bike and its rider heading to the handicap space in front of me.

"There she is, Miss America!" Mareck says, and he's all sound. His pants are lined with zippers and chains, pat-pat-patting against his legs. A thick one hooks from his wallet to his pants. He kisses me hard on the mouth, and I lick the taste of chocolate from my lips. I find pure anger starting to elbow out the fear in my throat.

"Just when I thought you couldn't get any sweeter," he says and grabs at my face with his eyes. They're an ungodly blue, and he measures my own two with them. "Hey, knock it off. I told you The Mule's just on her period. She's a liar, and you don't need to listen to her." He lets the bike slam to the ground, my bike that he "borrows" on a continuous loop. He holds me hostage in a bear hug.

Here's the problem: Leslie Buell or "The Mule" (as most of White Smoke calls her due to her unfortunate barn-like stature), has been spreading a rumor that she's "hooked up" with Mareck. I know that phrase can span a multitude of sins, but I don't get clarification from Mareck. I don't ask what really happened because I don't want to know what I already know.

I'm all alone.

He releases me, and I hug my coat even tighter. It's too thin and the faux fur trim is scorched off in places where a tweaking Mareck took a lighter to see if it would burn. Jerry keeps trying to buy me a new one, but Mom's strict about me not taking him up on any offers. Less guilt makes leaving easier, I guess.

I climb up on the handlebars and bite through the pain of cold metal through worn skirt. Marek wobbles onward onto Tully, and a backlog of cars pile up behind us. He's a mad Pied Piper, screaming the Beastie Boys on the top of his lungs and offering up one of his less honorable fingers. I almost fall off. Twice. There's anger there, but then there's also the jolt that jump starts my heart each time I feel like I'll fall to the pavement. My whole existence with Mareck has been like that, a constant undercurrent of loathing lifted in waves every time he shocks me. And that's why I never leave him. He's the only one who can bring me to life.

But sometimes, he says he might leave. He might head to Little Rock with his brother, Travis, and join the Bloods where his cousins rank on top. "White Smoke ain't no place for these good looks," he says, a smile bright against his milky brown skin. Half black, half white. He hasn't had the easiest time here where little minds seem to rule the roost. I get that. But I swallow down the possibility like a chalky horse pill and pray my stomach acid obliterates the idea.

Here's to hoping.

A car ride would be a neat five minutes to school but we get there thirty minutes later, six minutes late. We skid up to the front of the building, and I jump off, don't look anyone in the eye. It feels like a play, like I'm Juliet or the one I like better, Ophelia, and I'm taking my crazy to the stage. But none of the other stragglers applaud, just gape like fish even though they see me do this dance every single morning.

"Late," Principal Zinberg says, and he hands me and Mareck tired slips of paper from his pocket. Detention slips. They smell like sweat and boxer shorts.

We cattle call in with the rest of the last minute crowd and head to the locker we share. It's Mareck's, and it's against the rules to share lockers, but besides the soiled detention slips for arriving late or banning random attempts at religious freedom, no one really gives two squats about anything at White Smoke.

"Spanish, right?" Mareck says, and his blue eyes flash across my face. They're not a grown up's. They belong to a little boy, and that's what I like about the bits of blue and grey flecked tight into a ring. They make me remember we're still kids.

I nod, and Mareck kisses me on the mouth–another broken rule–and heads to his homeroom. I take the books I need and launch them into my empty backpack. I slam the door shut, and as I turn around, whose ugly mug is mere inches from my nose? Buell the Mule's.

Her face is nearly touching mine when she says, "See you around."

I hold tight to the words piling up behind my teeth. One detention slip is enough for today.

• • • •

CLASSES ARE MATCH-STRIKE fast because of my system. I sit in the back, which is the best place for people watching even if that means having to take in Jeremy Hunt shedding his dandruff with his long, dirty fingernails. Take for instance, Señora Howser's class. She's up there muttering in gibberish, smacking her doughy hand with an unsharpened pencil while I examine the back of Claudette Pinski's bubbly blond head. I match her up with Mr. Dandruff and draw in the blue-lined margin of my notebook what their baby would look like.

I know it's a weird thing to do, but I've got a thing for babies. Like Mom says, babies are what happen before life up and smacks you in the face.

So really, classes are just a blur of poorly drawn babies and dirty hair until it's lunchtime, and I find my phone without even realizing what I'm doing. It's cheap, like drug deal, prepaid burner cheap. Mom didn't even want me to touch the thing ("money's tight" being her favorite two words of all time), but she hates that I love Mareck and broke down and bought it on the off chance he bops me over the head and tries to cut me up into little pieces. I told him that part when we were camped out in his brother's truck, shoving pork rinds into our mouths while his brother, Travis, scored off some itchy white trash couple tripping for crank. He laughed a little too hard.

I take the phone and go to the bathroom, not the one on the ground floor where the seniors are packed sardine style but the one in the basement off the cafeteria that hardly anyone uses. I walk into the forbidden wheelchair stall that's unspokenly reserved for Melissa Stowe who lost a leg in a four wheeler accident last year. I lock it, slide my back down the cold tiled wall.

I text Mom: *Can we talk now?*

I stare in front of me, at the frank lime green streaks of paint covering the stall wall graffiti. It dings at me, the burner. *No, not yet,* Mom writes back.

That confirms it. I don't know how I know, but I do. Because when I read it, that simple-worded strand, it reminds me of when we left Texas after Dad died. How our whole lives became mere blips on nobody's radar.

The door slams open. There are two sets of feet, and I can tell they belong to two preps because they're fitted into ballet slippers, a silver pair and a purple. Their ankles are long, slender, and I think of my own in my dirty boots–thick as bricks. A genetic anomaly for a string bean.

"You can't be in the retard stall," a lazy voice says from one of them–maybe the silver pair–and I roll my eyes.

"Just leaving," I say and pop open the stall door, barely missing a short one with red hair. The girl's eyes go wide, and I know she's a freshman, which automatically means fun, and the fact that she's obnoxiously pretty will make it that much sweeter.

"Out of my way," I growl, and the girl backs up as I preen myself in the mirror. I do it for the girl's benefit–so she remembers my face–and for my own, too, so I can see what she's wearing and remember it for later when I'm lying in bed.

I do this thing where I think of the clothes I see The Preps wear and imagine what they'd look like on me. It's also a weird thing to do.

They huddle, the two of them–the other one taller but wider-eyed–and I laugh, a loud obnoxious laugh and try not to think about my fickle mother, my dead father, the boy who's never loved me. My damaged heart.

• • • •

THE MOST HORRIBLY PATHETIC thing about The Mule is that she's the most popular girl in school. And she really plays the part, like puts a ridiculous amount of effort into it. She's one of The Preps and has this purse she claims is a real Louis Vuitton, but all it looks like is a bottle of mustard and a diaper full of poop threw up on it. Her mom is the assistant manager of the Dairy Queen, and her dad is the sheriff, so there's no way that bag is real unless they've both lost their marbles. Which, by the looks of The Mule, I figure could be true.

"You've got this, you know. I mean look at you. You're short, but you're a scrapper. She gets that," Mareck says, rubbing the last centimeter of Chapstick against his lips. He texted me while I was in homeroom fifteen minutes before final bell. Fifteen minutes before we were both supposed to be in detention together. But Buell was calling me out, face-to-face, and the thing has to be settled.

"Sure," I say. He was supposed to have met me in the girl's locker room during lunch. We sit across from the shower stalls and pick at our food–another pudding cup for me, a bag of chips for Mareck. But he didn't show, and this is the third time in two weeks, and we just don't talk about it. I don't want to be a harpy, and I don't want him to be a liar. But then I think about the thing my psychology teacher's dropped on us more than once: reality exists regardless of whether you believe it or not.

After dodging Zinberg in the hall, we go outside and trek around the building to The Yard, me on the bars of my bike while Mareck heel-toes it along a patch of cold, dry earth. The Yard is basically a square inch of pavement reserved for the seniors. They can smoke out here and sit around making out or talk about keying the teachers' cars, but a lot of times it's used for a fight so they chain it up once the last bell rings. I jump over the gate.

The Mule is already there with two of her cohorts, Donkey and Horse Face. Those aren't their real names—one's Alice and the other starts with a "w" (Wanda maybe?)—but it's a lot easier to keep track of enemies when you label them appropriately.

"Little Wrennie. We were just talking about you. Ready to get the beating of a lifetime?" I have to admit, looking at The Mule, I believe she'll be doing just that. The Mule's tall—five-ten maybe—and her hands are kind of manly. The nails are painted though, a bright cherry red, and the sweater is knitted, navy with a tiny whale sewn into it above her right breast. I snapshot a memory for later.

"Cut it out, Leslie," I say. It comes out soft like I'm talking to a kitten. I hate my life.

"Cut it out, Leslie? That's all you got? You know what that jerk told me?" The Mule says, and she moves her beautiful blue sweater into my personal space. "He said you're nothing but a prude, and he just uses you for your money." She takes a step back to look at my face, and I give The Mule a full shot of me laughing. My money?

"Yeah, okay. That right Mareck? You all on me so you can hang out at my mansion?" My arms go wide like Jesus welcoming the little children, but when I turn around, Mareck is gone. And so is my bike.

"That's just awesome," The Mule laughs in my ear, and I think about all of it: my bike, Mareck strumming through my life with picky fingers. My mother's deep desire to flee and what she always says before we close up shop and head to the nearest Motel Six. *Don't worry. It'll all work out.*

And then before I know it, my fist is in The Mule's face, and there's a sharp pain currenting up my shoulder until it snaps inside my brain. I look down at my jacked up boots, a line of plaid skirt edging my knees and think, *Maybe it will.*

Chapter Fifteen
Natalie

Ten years ago, I got smacked in the face by a prostitute for sitting on "her" bench in our cozy little jail cell.

I guess you could say I'm now passing life with flying colors in comparison. But I know what it looks like. I know what Wren must think of me.

I just have a knack for not caring.

You ever go back in your head and look for *the* moment? The one where you snapped and everything changed around you? I guess if you were watching my life like a movie, you'd circle your red pen around the time I got arrested for illegally harboring somebody else's coke and nearly sending some Bronco owner to his early demise.

Good guess, but that's not it.

No. It's the day I was sitting in my kitchen, my husband next to me, years before Wren was even born. And I looked at his face, at the heart on his hand (which I always used to go back to as one of many reasons not to leave him. Who else would have the cajones to do something like that?), and I remember letting the voice talk to me for the very first time.

Natalie, we don't need any of this.

Sure, I used to think things like that all the time. Like when Rebecca was a snotty-nosed baby and would constantly tug at the end of my shirt. And I'd pick her up and hold her tight to my chest because it was something I had to do, and really, wanted to do, I guess.

But there was always that part of me that knew the difference.

That day at the kitchen table, though. That day? The voice wasn't mine. It was deeply sealed inside somebody else's chest.

Something else's.

It was the same voice that friended me during the dark nights and when I had to do something hard like leave everything I knew for Wren.

See, that's what she doesn't understand. How this was all for her.

It was the same voice that set me back on my feet and sent my fist flying into that prostitute's face, tit for tat.

Because if it were up to Natalie Reynolds, there'd be no fight. There'd be a deep sleep. A disconnect. And I don't know if you've looked around this life long enough, but the ones that check out are eaten alive.

It's the reason I still hate Rochelle so much.

She wasn't checked out. Okay, parts of her were. The part that knew her son, or more accurately, didn't. The part that turned a blind eye to her monster brother.

But with Wren. She loved Wren. She tried to teach her.

It's what she taught her that broke my heart.

Rochelle came up here to raise Wren. I won't act like that didn't mean something. My sister received the same opportunity, and I know she has Antonio, but I kind of feel like we lobbed the ball up for her to smash it out of the park. "I'm sure she has the means to find someone to take care of her daughter," is what she told the social worker. I've never bitten my tongue so hard. But then the social worker said Rochelle agreed and even wanted to move up here so Wren's life wouldn't be disrupted.

Saint Rochelle, I guess.

Man, I don't really mean that. It's just that while I was duking it out with that prostitute and then duking it out with Dr. Carol (first name, seriously) at the rehab center, Rochelle got to hold my daughter. And love her.

The very things I would have died to do.

But what also was a thorn in my already tired side was knowing how she took Wren to church. SHE. GOT. HER. BAPTIZED. I'm not gone but twelve months, and suddenly, I'm face-to-face with a goody two shoes who's been brainwashed to turn the other cheek.

I couldn't have that.

I couldn't let her be weak.

But here's the other thing: Rochelle was dying.

She didn't think to tell the social worker about that. About the breast cancer that was already eating her up, inside out. Selfish. That's what I thought. That's what I sometimes still do.

But maybe less selfish. Maybe more selfless.

Probably both.

How didn't she know that Wren would be torn to pieces? She waltzes back into her granddaughter's life only to teach her a fairytale and die.

And guess who's been handed the broom and dust pan?

Wren's a mess. I'm not blind. And I know the churchy folks will say, "It's because you ripped her away from her faith." She was seven. How does anyone know what they believe at that age?

I didn't hurt her. I helped her. And I have no regrets about it.

If I didn't do it, she wouldn't have survived.

She's strong now. A firecracker. She kind of reminds me of Mary which is worrisome but a better Mary. One that won't sizzle out. I caught wind that Mary died a few years back from "unknown causes."

She OD'd. I was right.

I'm always right about a lot of things.

The only thing that bugs the snot out of me is that Glenn never called to tell us that Rochelle died. I just never heard from her again. So poor Wren thinks I'm just on the outs with Rochelle and that the woman's still trucking along in Texarkana. And I refuse to call and prove her wrong.

But no matter. My girl's strong and no longer brainwashed by all that Jesus talk.

And she's going to be just fine.

Just like me.

"Hey there, sweet thing. You gonna come by and take my order or just tease me?" I look up and see a table of out of season hunters in camo coats and camo caps but mostly, I see dollar signs.

"Absolutely, baby," I say, discreetly hitching up my skirt an inch.

See? Just fine.

Chapter Sixteen
Rochelle

I didn't die.

That's the thing that I remember when I wake up every morning. You're here, and your limbs work, and God's talking to you. So get out of bed, lazy bones. Go make something of the day.

My heart rolls its eyes.

No, I didn't die, but I almost did. I did surgery and chemo and upchucked what felt like my stomach lining and lost a little bit of my soul. Not to mention my breasts (I had the option to reconstruct them, an option Glenn leaned heavily towards. And I'm ashamed to say maybe that's why I went the other route. Spite and whatnot).

My friends kept sending me Bible verses and baked goods and pictures of bald women hunched over with Jesus at their backs, touching them on their shoulders. And all of that was great but never made me feel any better. Because Wren was having her faith ripped away from her.

Natalie never said as much, but I saw what her eyes did when I told her Wren asked to be baptized.

It was a flash of something that wasn't her.

I left. I went back to Texarkana. I battled cancer and won. I battled Glenn and didn't.

Glenn was cheating on me. I knew it for a while, the whole time I was recovering, but I did something I've gotten pretty good at over the years: I compartmentalized. I put it back inside a little closet where my spine meets the back of my head, where memories of Dennis linger and that time my whole life was changed on some stranger's lawn.

My friends were concerned. I think my friend, Ann, was angry, but she didn't put it into words. Not at me, of course. I think at the whole idea of looking at a train wreck and not being given clearance to go clean it up. She spent a lot of time telling me the Lord is the only one I need to trust.

When I thought about it, I realized He was the only one I ever could.

But that didn't change the fact that Glenn was sleeping around. I was in bed watching Hallmark reruns, trying to fight off hot flashes from the chemo, and he was scoping out my replacement.

And now? He's started dating a twenty-two-year-old named Kimber(no -ly) who he found tending bar a few months ago at some karaoke place the firm takes their clients.

Nothing really surprises me anymore.

I took it to Jesus. I told Him I get it. All those years ago, He had given me a gift, my Mack. And I tended to him with one hand while the other was searching violently for another existence. Another circumstance. Because I didn't want to live in the now.

Which is really the only place you can.

Currently, I'm fully in the now. I've staked my claim on it, my fingers clawing into the soil. I went for a check up. Routine. Cancer's back. I wasn't surprised though. Because this is how a story always goes. You get time on the page and then God writes your ending.

But my heart's stopped rolling its eyes because God's now given me a few sentences to author. He's prompting me, I can feel it. The only person I see when I close my eyes is Wren. Something's wrong, and He needs me to revise it.

And I'm not going to disappoint Him.

Chapter Seventeen
Wren

While The Mule is mush on the ground, Alice and maybe-Wanda are hovering like flies around a dead body. They wouldn't have it in them to chase me anyways because they're nothing but talk. Also, Zinberg is standing on the sidewalk.

"What is this?" he says because he's too far away to see who's knocked out cold on the ground. The cohorts take that as their cue to flee, leaving their leader at my faux leather boots.

"Uh, nothing?" I call out as convincingly as possible. But Zinberg's ancient legs are swifter than I account for.

Even though it's January, and the world is nearly dead with cold, Zinberg is sweating as he sidles up next to me. His face is like a slick rubber ball with a weak mustache.

"Leslie Buell." He shakes his head. "Of all people," I think I hear under his breath. Apparently, I'm not the only one afraid of her. He lets out the air he's been holding in his chest and then takes out a cell phone, a burner like mine. I start to have visions of Hungry Man dinners for one and binge watching Cops in a recliner. I actually start to feel sorry for poor Zinberg.

"Elaine? Where are you? Parking lot? Already? Yeah, yeah I know it's final bell. Could you do me a favor? Leslie Buell's been knocked out cold here in The Yard. Yeah, I know. That's why I called. Appreciate it." He tucks the black plastic phone into his shirt pocket and assesses the damage, then me.

"Aren't you supposed to be in detention?"

I feel knotted, as if everything that makes me "me" has pretzeled in on itself. My arms are wrapped tight, and as the adrenaline wears off, I realize how cold I am.

"Sheh..." Zinberg says, running a hand through his thinning hair. He looks up at Nurse Elaine whose polyester pants are on the verge of starting a small fire. She's at The Yard now, peeking over the chain link fence before braving the gate's threshold.

"You weren't kidding," Nurse Elaine says. She takes The Mule's pulse with two fingers, and I study the nurse's dandruff on her black-belted coat. Her hair is fire engine red and crunchy with Aquanet. It's all I can do not to imagine the baby Nurse Elaine would have with Zinberg.

"Pulse is good. Sweetie, sweetie, this is Nurse Elaine. You've had a little...tumble. Can you hear me, sweetie? Can you get up?" Leslie's moving now, so at least murder charges won't be a part of my day. She starts to come to and is slowly helped to her feet by Nurse Elaine and Zinberg who takes her other elbow. I stand off to the side, out of The Mule's periphery as Elaine reaches down and grabs Leslie's Louis Vuitton. I imagine it tsk-ing at all of us.

"Leslie, Nurse Elaine is going to take you inside. She'll get you some juice and ice and call your dad," he says, seeming to choke a bit on the last word. Ah, Sheriff Daddy. No wonder he's trembling. Nurse Elaine gives him a "you owe me" look.

Inevitable, I think when Nurse Elaine and Leslie Buell have hobbled their way into the building. I drift between crying until I throw up and laughing like a maniac. As Zinberg moves closer to me, I take the third option: frozen and mute with fear.

"Where's that boy?"

"What?"

"The boy? The guy who never leaves enough room for the Holy Spirit."

"Um...Satan?"

"No...geez...the kid with you. Mark? Martin?"

"Oh. Marek. Yeah, he had better things to do. Like stealing my bike."

"He stole your bike? Isn't he your boyfriend?"

"That's the rumor," I say and automatically think of Mom. That bike was a portion of several paychecks, and even though I told Mom I didn't want one, she still bought it for me. "Can't get you a car, but I can give you this. A woman needs to know at least some freedom," she had said and then laughed a little. I could tell it tasted bitter in her mouth.

"Some boyfriend." He makes that "sheh" sound again and feels his hairline. "Alright. Follow me." I obey and follow behind like a spooked puppy dog. We walk through the side entrance, down the hallway to the heart of the school where a meager grouping of trophies is displayed in a case. White Smoke is legendary for getting our backside handed to us.

"This is me," he says as if I don't know which one is his office. I can practically hear a wolf howling as I enter it. It's the same pea green as the rest of the school, except instead of having the shiny tiled walls of the hallway, we're surrounded by rough cinder blocks. The mess is average, the odor, stale. And the little rotating fan near the window refuses to believe it's January, spitting wind in my face and the married stench of mold and body heat with it. I look back at Zinberg, and he's staring at the framed photo on his desk. It's a Sears special of him and his daughter, awkwardly hugging and staring into the camera. I almost forgot he had a daughter, a junior like me. They call her "The Kid."

"Take a seat." I do, and there's a rip in it that feels like it's devouring my leg.

"Lifelong enemy, I'm guessing? Stole your boyfriend?" Zinberg fishes a handful of Reese's Pieces out of a fake crystal bowl on his desk next to the picture. "Oh, where are my manners," he says, extending his hand to me. I shake my head "no" and wonder if I've entered some sort of twilight zone where Zinberg isn't a complete monster.

"Um, but yeah. Something like that."

"Do you go to church?" he asks. I look at him tweezing one of the candies with his fingers and then popping it into his mouth. As he chews, I notice his face is far less sweaty now. He's calmer and takes great care placing the candy into his mouth. I catch a glimpse of my kohl-lined eyes in the mirrored plaque on his wall and wonder if he's messing with me.

"I've been inside one." My Mimi always went to the small Baptist church in Texarkana. I'd go with her sometimes. It was the typical white clapboard affair. Pretty. Stale inside. Complete with a pastor who sneezed too much and seemed to share Zinberg's sweating disorder.

And then there was the time Mimi came to live with me. She took me to church and had me baptized. Sometimes, I close my eyes and remember the way the water felt, drowning to gain new life. I look around me. I've apparently let this one get a little moldy.

I want to call her. I want her to know everything because even though Mimi knows Jesus, she doesn't use him like a weapon. I think she'd understand but Mom thinks differently.

"Okay," he says, nodding his head like I gave the right answer. "Look, I'm going to switch things up. No more detention."

I perk up and watch him shovel another handful of candy-colored chocolate into his mouth. I'm starting to get my appetite back despite the visual.

"Really?"

"Instead, I want you to join The Cornerstone Club. My daughter's club." This is it, the catch. I watch what little reputation I had in the first place dissolve like wet ash down the kitchen drain. The Cornerstone Club is full of goody-goody losers who are involved in other just as dismal extracurriculars. Like chess club. It's led by The Kid whose ghost-white face stares back at me in the Sears photo.

I'll eat them alive.

"It's not as bad as you think. In fact, it's not bad at all. Think of it like a refuge, a safe haven. A place where nobody is stealing your bike." Zinberg looks like he's swallowing a small pile of stones. "Or your boyfriend."

He almost pleads with his raw blue eyes. I suddenly feel foolish in my rank smelling shirt and the skirt I keep pulling down with my sweaty hands. I feel like I'm wearing somebody else's uniform.

"Okay, I guess." I take the offer before he changes his mind. The Cornerstone Club will be a horrible, terrible punishment in its own right. But considering I just physically assaulted another human being on school grounds, I figure this a light slap on the wrist. "For how long?"

"The rest of the year."

Fine. A strong punch to the gut.

Chapter Eighteen
Natalie

Friday is Fry Day at Double Dees, half off all fried appetizers and entrees. So when I get off work, I smell like a hot vat of grease. I settle into the Pinto, the same rust bucket I drove up from Texarkana twelve years ago, and swat at the glove compartment door. Inside is a bottle of body spray. And that's it.

No more good time for Miss Natalie.

I spray it until I can taste it and then check my eyes in the rearview mirror. It's my favorite mirror because I can only see my irises and pupils and a small sliver of my face. I really don't have the desire to look at anything else.

I want to go to the apartment, but I don't want to face Wren. She texted me this afternoon, wanting me to spill. It's funny to me, the way things change. How all those years ago all I ever wanted was to come home to her, to tell her everything. But she's different now. I'm different. And I don't know how to face her and tell her what the pregnancy test in the employee bathroom at Double Dee's has already confirmed.

I'm having a baby.

But I really can't have a baby.

I knew something was up when I started retching at the number five chili dog platter a few days ago. I started to do the math in my head but gave up on that little endeavor seeing that I like to black out anything that's ever happened before today.

One of Dr. Carol's infamous survival tips.

At least I know who the father is which is a dismal victory. Jerry's great. Jerry's the level-headed supportive type who pays his bills. Jerry thinks I'm a goddess.

But Jerry's not the father.

And anyways, he's no Mack, and therein lies another part of the problem.

Another thing Dr. Carol said before I graduated from rehab is that I have an issue with keeping the past in the past. The second thing is that I make idols of dead people.

Mack. Mary. And most recently, Rochelle.

But what I could never convince Dr. Carol of is that I didn't seek them out, dead or alive. One day, each one just became a part of my life. And they never had the courtesy to leave.

I turn down Shepherd heading back to the apartment, but before I do, I stop at Floyd's. The after 5 crowd has thinned out, and I wish to all things holy this town was self-respecting enough to feature a drive-through liquor store. But I don't go in anyways. I just sit in the parking lot and strain my vision through the window, side skirting an advertisement for freshly made nachos to look at the refrigerators lined with beer. I'm so desperate that I'm willing to stare at beer at a gas station when I only ever used to drink vodka.

I laugh at that, and then I cry at that and all the other things I've stored inside of me worth crying about. I leave the parking lot and head back home.

Home. Now that's a joke if I've ever heard one.

Chapter Nineteen
Rochelle

When I was cleared and categorized as "cancer-free," I decided to leave Glenn. I had known about Kimber for the past two weeks because I followed him at night. It was disgusting to see a man that old with a girl that young (and Kimber is nothing if not a girl). But then I looked at things from Glenn's "deep" world view: my wife is decaying, I'm getting old, I need to be taken care of.

Because I don't care what anyone says. Glenn Augustus has loved me for a long time, so lack of it wasn't the problem. The problem was Glenn's fear and the way he let it destroy everything else.

Another problem might have been the mirror, more specifically me in it. Chest flat and war-scarred. Hair wispy and cut close to the scalp. I don't even wear makeup anymore. I'm sure he thinks it's my version of holding up my middle finger, but really, it's my version of getting used to who I am outside of somebody else's expectations. And I know it's hard for someone like Glenn to no longer call the shots.

So I let him come to me and confess. I was patient and kind, and when I told Ann all that had happened, she wore the look of horror and frustration for me. But I can honestly say I didn't feel those things. I wasn't passive either, but I didn't beg him.

I let him make his own choice. Something I wish we'd all let each other do a little more of.

I suppose that's also the reason I haven't reached out to Natalie these past ten years. In the beginning, she sent pictures scattered in the mail. Wren at school, Wren at the park. They seemed tentative; no note attached. Just a mandatory chore checked off the list. And then they stopped completely.

She seemed unsure of herself, which I know is most certainly the case.

When I had first met Natalie, I was thoroughly impressed but that might have been because I only had my son to compare her to.

It was like comparing apples to very bruised oranges.

She seemed to have her life together, and when I learned she had raised her younger sister, it hadn't surprised me. Natalie was the type with a good head on her shoulders.

Even Glenn mentioned she seemed like a stellar girl. I was too naive to understand the motive behind his compliment at the time, but at least we agreed.

After knowing everything she'd been through–Mack's death, the funeral, changing her entire life to chase something the rest of us couldn't even see–I was floored when I got the call from the social worker. Natalie? Our Natalie?

She had become an alcoholic. Something I guess Mack was, but I had never known. Not until I was able to get her on the phone and ask her what had happened. At this point I had just received my diagnosis, so angry was something I was well-versed in. But I didn't let her feel it in my voice. I kept my cards close and my hurt even closer.

"What do you think, Rochelle? His life wasn't exactly rosy, you know. He had a lot going on, especially in his childhood." She stressed the last word, a pointed dagger at my heart. I didn't resist it, but I didn't pull her fist into my chest either.

"I'm so sorry," is all I said because I was. Thinking of my granddaughter, of the burdens she'll carry because of the decisions all of us have made. How is that fair?

And yet, how is it not? We're all aware of consequence. We're all aware of the hammer that comes crashing down when we get it all wrong.

But what Natalie didn't know–and most likely still doesn't–is the depth of God's mercy. How he hovers and weaves through all of us.

He covers our bad hearts, our bad choices.

He sparks the violent hope inside our bellies that one day, things will be different.

Because with Him, they always are.

Chapter Twenty
Wren

I walk all the way home. I let the cold work through my skin and bones and don't even flinch when a kid in a bright green car drives by and gives me the finger. My mind is as numb as my body is. As numb as my heart.

Marek stole my bike.

Marek stole everything.

I walk-run for a little bit until I'm on Shepherd, and there's a lot of after school stragglers hitting the arcade, the pizza shop, standing and smoking outside of Floyd's Gas Stop, getting high off the fumes. There are massive canvas flags, stained red with razorbacks because everyone loves football, and a guy with a gut the size of a 'roided out watermelon fingers them like they're fine china. I walk past him into Floyd's because I always like it here. The bathroom overtakes the smell of gasoline when you walk in, and there's this display of lamps, replicas of the one from *A Christmas Story*. Fishnet legs lighting up a room. The absurdity is everything that's right with this world, and if I had the cash or could swipe one without guilt swallowing me like a snake, I'd be able to stare at it every night until my eyes hurt. But I don't have the cash. I don't even have my stinking bike.

I do have dirty change rattling in my coat pocket and choose a Pay Day for the sheer irony of it although I'm not even sure I'm using that word correctly. Mrs. Brentwood went into this whole spiel about irony once and the devastating way Alanis Morissette pretty much just slaughtered the word and then someone piped up with, "My mom said Alanis used to date Dave Coulier, so I reckon her judgment has always been pretty fried," and from there, I zoned out of Lit class and drew what I imagined Alanis Morissette and Dave Coulier's baby would look like. It wasn't very pretty.

"Which one you thinking, baby?" A voice strikes hard at me like a stone from a sling. I rise on tiptoe and search the next aisle. Mareck is with something redheaded and giggly. As I crouch down, I clutch the PayDay like a throat.

I stretch up again to watch the top of the giggler's head cock with the life changing decision of Bugles or CheezIts. Mareck comes up from behind her. Gooses her. The sound she makes ice picks my ear. I get a better view hip to hip with the soda fridge and see Mareck touch the girl's sweatered back. She's a prep, a freshman prep. And then she turns, and her face is gorgeous, and I realize this at the exact same moment Mareck does except that his lips kiss the giggler's and mine just stupidly tremble.

It's The Redhead from the bathroom.

I bet they'd make a beautiful baby.

I leave with the unpaid for Pay Day in my hand, but I'm not stopped because I reek of unfiltered pathetic, and no one wants to catch a whiff of that.

Outside someone whistles at me. It's long and drawn out and belongs to a man around my Grandpa Glenn's age, and I lick my lips at him. I hate when I do things like that, but there's a switch somewhere beneath my breastbone, and when one of Mareck's dirty fingers flips it on, there's just no stopping me.

I lift my skirt a little, show off a pale strip of leg, and the old man's face grows a smirk. I stand there for a second then reach between my ribs to finger the switch and shut it off. I turn and snap tight the silver buttons running up my brown coat. I rub the bare spots in the fur out of habit. When the man's lost interest, I walk a little further from Floyd's and fish my glue bottle out of my boot. It fits snuggly against my skin and has walked with me like a friend all day, hand-in-hand while I nursed my anger and put my fist through The Mule's face. The last image causes me to take an extra long whiff.

A gap widens through my thoughts, a nice comfy spot for Dad to saunter in, and he sits down, elbowing Mareck's brittle bones and The Mule's much more substantial ones out of the way. He asks, "Wrennie, what happened?"

"I could ask you the very same thing," I say. I walk, and it's hell to walk. It's getting colder, and I realize nobody thought to grab my backpack I left in The Yard.

Fantastic.

"You could," Dad says, and there he is in front of me, head in his hands. Sympathy card, but I won't let him play it. Walking in these boots is a blister waiting to happen, but I have no other option. I could jam out my thumb, but with my luck I'd be picked up by Principal Zinberg and have to suffer through his silent farting and spiel on pants being more suitable for the cold. I guess he isn't all bad considering I'm not locked up in some federal prison right now. He almost seemed...empathetic.

I walk heel-toe for a while with my arms spread out like an airplane. I'm honked out, and receive a "Watch it, stoner!" from a beat up minivan. Dad waits for me to look him in the face, his chin up now, eyes horrified as I dance around a mailbox like it's a pole.

"Don't worry. I don't take my clothes off for money. I do it for free," I say.

"What are you proving?" he asks. He's dressed like I remember him. Jeans, gray hoodie, and his faded leather jacket on top. The heart on his hand looks like it's bleeding.

I lie sometimes when I talk to him, but then I think of Mareck, The Redhead, even The Mule and The Kid in her stupid Cornerstone club– all of them fitting comfortably in their niches when I'm crammed tight and can't even move to breathe.

"That one day someone, something will try to hurt me, and I won't even be able to feel it," I whisper. The last look is how it usually goes, his eyes closed because that's how I remember him mostly now from the time he hovered angel high above my head. I was the one who found him in the tree.

I put the tiny glass bottle of glue in my thick sock, jam it down into my boot. I have two more in the hidden drawer of the jewelry box Mom bought me the day I got my period. It's floral patterned and smells funny because Mom found it at a garage sale, so it belonged to someone who was okay with that smell, and the whole notion is perplexing. In fact, everything's perplexing because I'm gliding, skating across the street until I'm stepping on the sidewalk and climbing up the apartment stairs. God is my friend today because Mom's not here yet. I sneak into our apartment unscathed, commandeer a pudding cup and let my hungry belly lead me to my room.

Mom does come home at some point, and I yell something about being sick, about leaving me alone even though that's the last thing I'd ever want. And maybe that's because I figure one day, it will probably come true.

I dream snippets: me alone, Mareck laughing, The Redhead stealing my glue. Mom's not there, not even Dad, just me and these faces, balloon-like, asking why I've made a mess of myself and me too high to answer.

So I sleep, not really sleeping because my mother and Jerr-bear finally go to their room and challenge the paper thin walls. Mom's hushed tones, Jerry's not-so-hushed crying. It sounds like death, and I almost wish it were.

Because breathing? It hurts like the devil.

Chapter Twenty-One
Natalie

Here's what happened: I was arrested and went to court. I was sentenced to rehab and an insurmountable fine that Glenn Augustus begrudgingly (I can only assume) paid, and Rochelle came up and changed my daughter without my permission. I also received a lovely severance letter from JCC.

I was in there for a year. It was no Betty Ford. There was no pool or hot tub or sessions with a masseuse who could work my problems right out of me. There was food that tasted like cardboard, and for whatever reason, lunch and dinner was served with a broccoli cauliflower mix that made my eyes water. Dr. Carol wasn't ominous or a pain in the rear or anything. She was just doing her job. And she did teach me a lot about myself, whether I wanted to hear it or not.

After the first three months, Wren was allowed to visit me. I wanted to see her alone, but Rochelle never got that hint. I could sense something in her. She'd claw her hand around Wren's shoulder and stiffen her lip. I was the enemy. The bad monster who would wreck her precious granddaughter.

How easily Rochelle forgot that Wren was mine.

I vowed to get better. No more alcohol. It just wasn't an option. And I had to get all the anger out of my head so I wrote letters to Mack, Dennis, Rochelle, and Mary that Dr. Carol helped me burn. I wrote one to Wren that I still have in the back of my closet.

All these things didn't make me feel one iota better. But I was really good at pretending they did.

When I got out, Rochelle went home. She tried to stay. She tried to make it seem like I'd need her to get back on my feet when all I really needed was for her to leave us alone.

I didn't know about the baptism until right before she flew home, and Wren chimed in, telling me she'd been dunked in a cold tank of water.

"And how did that make you feel?" I asked after Rochelle had finally left, channeling my innermost Dr. Carol.

"Good. It's because of Jesus," she said, and I tried to keep from gnawing holes in my cheeks.

"Oh, is that right? You know, Wren, sometimes adults have us do things that we might not want to do. You don't have to go back to that church anymore," I said, applauding how progressive I was. We weren't going to let the past or bad religion determine our fate. In fact, I was pumping myself up to call up my old boss, Tara, at JCC and get my job back. Dr. Carol would vouch for me. And as she pointed out, I hadn't changed. If anything, I'd been renewed. Whatever that meant.

"But I want to go."

"Oh honey, you're too young to know what you want," I whispered gently in her ear.

From that point on, that was something only I and I alone would determine.

Chapter Twenty-Two
Rochelle

Kimber eventually moved in with us.

Ann thought this was ridiculous.

"Godless heathen," she had said in my car after my diagnosis and the odd course my life was taking was starting to sink in. I played with the windshield wipers even though it wasn't raining. My old constant, my Jaguar, something I had always wanted and worked my tail end off for even though I hadn't saved enough when Glenn had generously bought it for me. But the sentiment was there. My will to work my fingers to the bone was there. My will to keep going no matter the cost.

"That's not Christian," I said.

"Neither is she." I smiled at Ann. Ann with the good heart and passion deeper than any I've ever harbored. Ann used to be an atheist. And before that she lived with a hippie and practiced free love. And before that her god was a tiny razor she kept in her make up case to cut at her arms when she got stressed out. Which, I once pointed out, was pretty forward thinking of her considering that wasn't even a fathomable thing in the fifties.

"You know, some would say you were once a godless heathen. And now look at you."

"I was a trailblazer," Ann said. Ann had (and still does) a fervor for God that can only come from someone who's lived a lifetime on the other side of the coin. And I'm thankful she's my friend. "And some would say it takes one to know one," she had added, pretending to figure out how the cigarette lighter worked when Kimber spotted us in the car.

"I know, which only means I'm qualified." I smiled and squeezed Ann's hand. She sat in the passenger side with a straw brim hat on her head and a flowery sleeveless blouse. It's like she purposely picked out her clothes to flip off her old life.

"Really, why are you letting him do this to you?" She meant why I was allowing Glenn to move his new girlfriend into our home. I hadn't even filed for divorce yet. We sat, the sun hitting off the Jaguar's nose and watched as Kimber pointed and shouted orders to the movers. For someone who lived in a studio apartment, she was rife with junk.

"Can I cite that bit about turning the other cheek?"

"He said to turn the other cheek, not to let your replacement move in." Now Ann was the one squeezing my hand. "I'm sorry, Ro."

"It's okay, Ann." After sitting and staring and pretending to be figuring out how the A/C in my car worked every time Kimber would look our way, Ann got into her own car and drove home. I stayed out in mine a little longer.

I wanted to go inside. But I stayed until the sun went down, not because Kimber was inside or Glenn. It was because there was a change God had waiting for me. And at this point, I wasn't sure I was strong enough to weather it.

Chapter Twenty-Three
Wren

Waking up is always the hardest part of the day. It involves breaking through the dark to the light, and there's too much of it streaming through the crack in my black curtains. My eyes open to my popcorn ceiling, and I have the same thought I have every morning: I wonder what it would taste like with a little butter.

And then I remember last night. Avoiding Mom, getting too high. Forcefully sleeping through the dull cramp in the back of my head reminding me Mareck's gone. I feel under the covers and curse under my breath. I've peed my bed again, a downside of needing to go and being too high to do anything about it.

The bathroom mirror confirms it: I'm a urine-soaked mess. There's a wide breadth of limp skirt material belting around my hips. My hair is making fun of me, ringing around in jet black curly cues so I look like a half-dead Barbie doll, and any which way I turn, it's pretty obvious that there's no winning in this situation. So I step into the shower's steam and soap up, washing away the glue, the urine, The Mule and her blackened face and Mareck and his ugly heart. I ignore my pin thin thighs, my chest that's "flatter than an ironing board" as one of my classmates once so gallantly put it.

I make a better boy than most boys.

I feel better, though, in the muggy seven-by-seven room and wipe a hole in the fogged up mirror. My face, small, a peckish little hen of a nose sitting defiant and two eyes ringed with leftover mascara, not grey but not green, looking through me. In this game of chicken, I blink first. I find my eyeliner in my junky makeup drawer and go to work.

Back in my room, I stash my defiled t-shirt and underwear into a plastic bag I found in the dense waste under my bed. I change into a tight pair of jeans with safety pins saddled up the sides. The t-shirt is white, nearly threadbare. One I should wear a bra under, but I don't.

I walk through the empty apartment with my laundry bags. Jerry and Mom work weekends, so I'll have the apartment to myself. Usually my plans are already made. Mareck comes by. Mareck watches our TV. Mareck eats our food. Mareck goes too far with me, and I regret everything I do with him which is stupid because I know girls who do far worse. And why should I feel guilty anyways? It's not like there's anyone here to judge.

Mareck eventually goes home, and then I smile through dinner with Mom and Jerry who tells us about the crazy people and their broken A/Cs. Once, a lady offered him cat food as a snack. The thought is one I easily climb, thinking of Jerry and his lovable face graciously turning down a feline treat. I grab Mom's oversized Razorbacks sweatshirt and put it on for his sake.

Today, there will be no Mareck. I wipe hard at the thought like a smudge, letting my anger eat at my hurt. At least it's Saturday now which is a small gift from the gods. Maybe in two days The Mule will forget all about our little tiff out in The Yard.

Maybe I should change my identity and move to Mexico.

I think about a chocolate pudding cup, but the stench from my laundry is thick enough to eat, so I skip breakfast and head to the laundry room in our complex.

The cold hurts but snaps me awake, and I can see through the glass double doors that the laundry room's practically empty. Inside, I pretend to read a magazine until the fat lady with her load of whites has folded the entire lot. She walks with a limp and frowns at me like it's my fault her legs don't work.

I take off one of my boots and dump out a sad tinkling of coins after the lady leaves. Then I start in on my search, first the tiny coin compartment in the vending machine, digging upward and onward until I'm scared I'll lose a finger. Next, under the bench smashed against the wall. I find a quarter crammed behind one of the legs and retrieve my find along with a thread of web and a baby spider.

Yelping and smacking my hands on my pants, I'm thankful that the laundry room is empty. But then I turn around.

The Kid is staring at me slack-jawed with her hand held out. The Kid is small, half my size small. There's a rumor at school that she was a preemie and was supposed to die but decided it just wasn't the right time.

"For the love of Moses," I say. The Kid takes her hand and helps me to my feet. For the first time ever, I feel like a young baby giraffe looking down on a blade of grass. The Kid wears a blue pea coat, and in the crack where the sides of it should meet, I see she's wearing her typical garb: black sweatpants, the kind that choke off your ankles and an oversized tee-shirt with the words "Frankie Says Relax," whatever that means. The Kid's smart, the smartest kid in our class, but she dresses like she doesn't believe it.

"What are you doing here? You don't live here do you?" I dart my eyes around the room, preparing myself for a Zinberg run-in.

"No. Dad told me you'll be joining Cornerstone. I wanted to welcome you."

"On a Saturday?" I ask, hit with the sudden panic that my laundry smells like human waste, so I go to dump my bags in an empty washer.

"Yeah, well, Saturdays are the cornerstone of Cornerstone. So to speak." The Kid is eyeing the place like she's scared to touch anything. I don't blame her. The laundry room at Legends Apartments is a decorative blend of mental hospital meets torture chamber.

"They have a real knack for ambiance around here," I say, following The Kid's gaze. "It's legendary...so to speak."

"Mmm...hmmm." There's something more written on The Kid's face but I don't probe. I wait until she gathers enough courage to let me have it. "He's a tool. He shouldn't have stolen your bike."

I snort, shove in the change after adding a whopping dollop of somebody's nearly empty Tide they left on a dryer. "That just another one of your spy tactics? Or did daddy give you my life story?" I feel kind of bad I say it and try avoiding The Kid's eyes. But I can't because the girl has the saddest, palest blue eyes in the world. They don't even have the decency to cover the truth up.

"I was out in our car in the parking lot, waiting for Dad. I know what happened." The Kid's face looks like mine should: disappointed in the world. But I'm shocked anyone else–besides the handful of both conscious and unconscious people at The Yard–know about Mareck. I'm surprised anyone else cares.

"Yeah, well, he's got a lot on his plate right now."

"That so?"

"I don't know. Ask him yourself. You seem to be terribly interested in him for whatever reason." I go and sit on the bench where The Kid found me on hands and knees. She sits right next to me.

"Why are you really here?" I ask. We're both hunched, the big and little versions of each other. The air smells like detergent and a used diaper that hasn't been properly disposed of. The Kid rolls around options in her head and looks me in the eye again. "I thought you could use a friend."

I snort again, this time quieter. I've never really had a friend. When we first moved to White Smoke, there was one girl, my mom's friend's daughter. But I don't remember a lot about her. And besides, I grew up and learned what everyone else already knew about me: I was nothing more than trailer trash. So it was just me for a while until the first day of freshman year when it became me and Mareck. And so losing him isn't just losing a small spark of love. It's losing hope, too.

I stretch and think about it for a second, trying my best to ignore The Kid's blue eye attempting to catch me in her periphery. I figure maybe an adventure would get me out of my head. And if anything goes south, there's a bottle of glue ready to help dry my tears. "Well, friend.

We better get going then," I say, hand extended, and I feel the bones in The Kid's shockingly small one.

"Sure. But one thing."

"What?"

"Call me Rhonda."

Chapter Twenty-Four
Natalie

I work Saturday mornings. I work all the time.

But not Saturday afternoons.

In the afternoon, I'm off. I want to go back to the apartment, but I know Wren will be there with that Mareck, the boy who will ruin her life because that's what men do. I warned her, but of course, a warning from a sound, reasonable human being only added fuel to their juvenile fire.

I have to let her make her own mistakes, I suppose.

I want to go to a bar although I hate bars. I settle instead for the TGI Fridays in Junction, still in my Double Dees outfit. It's a real doozy. Short shorts with tights and knee-high boots. My top is cut too tight, a powder blue with "Double Dees" in curly script. I'm wearing my black trench coat, though, which I'm sure looks like I'm covering up something even more risqué. But it's one-thirty when I finally roll up, and the lunch crowd has thinned out. This is where I typically go. I leave the subpar restaurant I work at for a gimmicky chain, and I sit in a booth. My legs are thankfully covered so I can't feel the stickiness of the seat. But still, I imagine them, all the people who have sat there over the years and wonder who's alive and who's dead.

I don't have a lot of other hobbies.

When my broccoli cheddar soup comes lightly bobbing in the hands of "Tiffany" (who's treating me a little like I've escaped the local insane asylum), I dig into it, looking for answers. Wren asked me once why her daddy killed himself, and I look for that answer but can't find it. Rochelle asked me once why I had to be so selfish, dragging her grandchild to "who-knows-where-ville." Can't find that one either. I keep digging but nothing comes to me, not even at the end of the bowl when I've eaten everything inside but feel even emptier than when I started.

By phone buzzes. A text: *Meet soon?*

I don't even wipe my hands or mouth before I type my reply: *Of course.*

I pay Tiffany and give her a twenty percent tip. I know what it's like–your feet sore, your back sore. Life pinning you between a plate full of cheesy fries and some customer's bad breath.

She's looking at me like I'm a little less crazy now.

In my car, I spray Binaca into my mouth and absorb a mist of body spray. I brush my hair and check my mascara. I rub a glob of gloss against my lips. When Wren was little, I liked playing games with her. At the time, I thought it was a good way for her to process things, to cope with the wild world we were chaotically flung into. Rochelle would have called it "organized chaos." A journey we take to grow like we're flowers or some other nonsense.

Thing is, weeds grow, too.

I would hide and Wren would come and find me, and every time her face was so happy. She knew I hadn't left the apartment. She knew I was somewhere deep inside the shallow space. But no matter. When she saw me, she loved me, and her face showed every ounce of it.

I haven't seen that face in a long time. And I'm starting to think I don't deserve to.

I show up to the condo but park around back. I check my favorite mirror again, studying my face in sections. *Things are expensive*, I tell myself like I always do.

I open the car door and walk around the block. I stick out like a sore thumb, a black thumb in my trench coat. I take care not to slip and slide on the sidewalk, icy in patches where concrete meets grass. I take a deep breath before I push the doorbell of 103. I ignore the "Welcome" sign which would turn its face if it realized the kind of person it was welcoming.

The door opens and my boss, Hootie, answers with a slimy smile on his face. "Right on time," he says.

"Always am." I go in deeper and deeper into the shallow condo and wish somebody would come find me.

Chapter Twenty-Five
Rochelle

Ann offered me a place to stay. I turned her down, and she didn't say a word. I'm sure she expected the answer.

I didn't tell the rest of the group about Kimber. Marjorie got to the point in our meeting for prayer requests, and I could feel Ann and her hatless head boring into me. But it doesn't make for a great group conversation. Even if I could use all the prayers I can get.

I don't sleep in his room anymore. Our room, I guess. It was my idea to move out so I wouldn't have to hear him say the words.

"You sure?" he asked. I don't know what I was expecting. That he would realize what he was ending and tell Kimber to get out. I knew that wasn't going to be the case. When you can't see life from Jesus's point of view, anything goes. It's in our DNA. It's still in mine even though I've been bought and paid for. So who am I to judge him?

I guess that's what I have a hard time verbalizing to Ann. She's the one with the wild past. But I've never been able to tell her how dirty mine is.

So I sleep now in one of the guest rooms. And I guess that's all I'm really doing. Sleeping, barely eating, using the toilet, praying. Surviving.

I wonder what Kimber thinks. Ann says thinking most likely isn't one of Kimber's strong suits. But I know the girl must sense this is all a mess. So I'm going to ask her. I'm going to make her my friend.

To Glenn, she's just a young girl who wants sex and a sense of power, but that's selling the girl short. Because I see her eyes sometimes when I'm on the couch reading, and she's doing her best to avoid me. There's shame there.

A sense of wrong.

And Lord help me if that isn't more than I ever had.

Chapter Twenty-Six
Wren

The place smells like canned peaches inching past their sell by date. The dining room is settling down, breakfast now coming to a hard close at 10 o'clock. I ignore the strained rumbling in my stomach and then ignore the fact that old peaches are the cause of it. Maybe I can find a pudding cup to swipe.

"Rhonda Zinberg, Cornerstone Club." The aid at the round desk in the foyer nods Rhonda through. It would be impressive if she wasn't wearing a sweatsuit like a four-year-old and this wasn't an old folks' home.

"There's someone you need to meet," Rhonda says. I follow her down the hallway lined with doors. The names on them feel old time Hollywood: Montgomery, Hazel, Edith. The smell is less peaches now, more old age and ointment. My heart beats its bird wings. I feel ridiculous, a combination of marching to the guillotine and finding the answer to a life gone wrong.

Maybe I'm still high.

"Here." Rhonda says. She doesn't go in. She doesn't knock on the door. "Think you'll be okay?"

"What? You want me to just go in? By myself?" Rhonda rolls her eyes and looks down

the hall. There's a nurse coming out of the room next door.

"Hi. My, uh..." Rhonda looks at me, assessing what it is exactly she's looking at. "My...friend would like to visit Mrs. Ling. Do you mind announcing her arrival?" I start to panic, and then there's the embarrassment worming through my veins. I should have worn better pants.

"Sure," the nurse says with a plastic smile. She walks over and opens the door with brisk force. "Knock, knock. Mrs. Ling? I have someone to see you."

I look for Rhonda who's already down the hall and giving me a meager thumbs up.

"Won't you please come in?" There's a small wisp of a woman drinking tea, her Bible opened next to the saucer. I look uncertain, feel uncertain. I worry if I walk through the door, I'll burst into flames.

"Don't be afraid. I don't bite as much as I used to." I walk forward as the nurse chuckles and closes the door behind me. I cover the holes in my jeans with my hands.

"Sit. Sit. I'm Eleanor," Eleanor says with a faint Chinese accent that's been left in the wash too long. I do what she says because old people make me feel nervous. At least my legs are hidden under the table cloth.

"First time? Cornerstone Club?" Eleanor stops talking so I can nod at her. "Rhonda dear is such a legend around Morningside. Nobody really cares what happens to us in here. But those kids do thanks to her." Eleanor rubs the pages of her Bible with an absent mind.

"I didn't choose to join. I was forced." *Might as well tell the old bag the truth*, I think. Nobody's going to mistake me for someone who does community service for funsies.

Eleanor laughs. It's soft and muffled by a swallow of tea. "Honesty. The best policy. It also helps to determine if I like you or not. I think I do."

"Well, I'll at least have someone in that category." I trail off and look around. The room's warm with sage on the walls and thick almond colored carpet on the floor. We're seated at a round, wooden table against the wall, two chairs only. There's a small couch and chair complete with a coffee table and a small kitchenette standing quietly behind them. The wall opposite has a chest of drawers working double duty as a TV stand and there's a door to the right of it, slightly ajar. Eleanor's room.

Old people have all the luck, apparently.

"My son. My son, he's the one who did all this," Eleanor says as her eyes trail along the room with mine. "He has a good job, good wife, and kids. I suppose though that's in spite of me. Not because of." I stop trailing and land on Eleanor's face. The woman isn't lying about honesty.

"I can't imagine you were a bad mother." Mom is there again in my head. I'll talk to her later in the evening when she's peeled off any trace of Double Dees and Jerry is out bowling with his team. I'll nod and pretend to understand because if I don't, Mom's bound to lose it like she sometimes does. And I'll plead with her, remind her that we can't afford a place on our own. How much easier to just weigh the stakes and marry Jerry. How much easier to just try and have a family even if it looks a little different than it used to.

But Mom's in love with a dead man.

It's the one thing I can't fix.

"*Bad* comes in all shades. All colors. It's born when you're born and lives like a little seed inside your belly. You can grow it or you can give it over. I grew it for a long, long time." Eleanor bends her head to take another sip. The sprouts of gray hair that have escaped her bun wave at me.

"Is that like a haiku or something?"

"No, haikus are Japanese. Don't be racist." The burn is immediate in my face until I see Eleanor's eyes laughing at me. "I thought your kind was, what's the word? Chill?" She laughs, this time freed from her tea cup, and it's a light and beautiful sound.

"I'm not sure *chill* has ever been the word to describe me."

"Then what's the word?"

"Damaged." It slips out, only to serve my theory that I must still be high. The burn's back. I look down at my thighs, the skin escaping through denim bars.

"Damaged. Well, you're going to have to share your stock in that one. One time I punched a wall so hard, I fractured my middle finger. I could no longer punch. I could no longer offer the bird. I had to learn to use my words." I'm pretty sure my eyes are black-ringed saucers.

"Why? What happened?"

"Oh, nothing short of a typical day, I'm sure. Let's see. Sticky-handed children who loved me. Patient husband who loved me. They just weren't a part of my plan. I mean, I suppose they were, but I wanted one of those. Oh what's it called? Do over? Yes. I wanted a do over." Eleanor strokes at the thin pages of her Bible again. "There is no such thing, though. There is only here and now and whether you're willing to stack it all in your hands or not. I wasn't. So I punched." I'm alarmed to see the tears in Eleanor's eyes. I feel trapped in a huge vat of awkward.

"Tim. My husband. He iced my hand. He said 'There, there, Eleanor. No more sad.' And for Tim, it was that easy. But I don't know if that man really understood." A tear slips, moves down to her mouth. I look back at my thighs. "It becomes a part of you. It hardens all the organs, and if you ignore it, it won't ignore you. There's no giving it away. Or so I thought." I think of my anger. The way it braids through me like hair.

"You were wrong?" I find the courage to ask it, eyes still on skin and jean.

"I had been wrong my whole life," Eleanor says, and I sip the truth like tea.

• • • •

"SO, MRS. LING?" I CAN tell Rhonda tries to ask it casually as she noses out of Morningside's parking lot. I don't feel like talking. I feel like sniffing glue until I pass out.

"She's okay," I lie. Mrs. Ling is more than okay. She's like a box I'm forbidden to look into, but I do anyways. And what I see is sun and light and concrete. Because I feel my heart break out of me, just a little bit. But that feeling comes to a halt when I think of Dad's dangling feet.

"The woman changed my life," Rhonda says.

"That so?" I say, lost in the thoughts outside my window. "So every Saturday, huh?"

"Mostly, yeah. Meetings every Monday. I try to do a once a month thing where we all hang out. Eat pizza. You know, be kids or whatever."

"Oh. Wonder what that feels like." My head against glass, I watch the trees spin by, pretend they're magnolias.

I press an inconspicuous hand to my face, drying the tears on my right cheek. Mrs. Ling is free from her shame, I can see that much. But there's still a hurt there from letting her children down. I think of Mom and smirk. *Misery loves company.* The phrase passes through like a whisper in my skull. I look over at a frowning Rhonda. I smirk again.

Chapter Twenty-Seven
Natalie

Things are expensive, I hear in my head. It's the broken record that's been playing since the first time I first walked into the condo Hootie shares with his wife and two kids. "Summer last year," he had said, giving a hard nod at the picture of the four of them at Branson on the wall. I hadn't asked and didn't care. His life is inconsequential.

Our arrangement began the day I walked into his office to apply for the waitressing position. I know when a man is interested, and to say Hootie was interested is an understatement. I practically had to swat him off me like a fly my first day at Double Dees. He didn't officially ask to start seeing me at his place until the end of my first shift, probably making sure I was adequate enough to wait tables and not punch any of our customers in the mouth.

The part where I get paid for my side gig? That was all me.

"Like a prostitute?" Hootie had asked the first time I set foot inside his key lime colored condo. The whole development was meant to give a Calypso vibe like you're in the middle of the Bahamas and not right across from the paper processing plant. The scent in the air is definitely not reminiscent of an ocean breeze.

"No. Like someone who's risking her reputation and career so her boss can get his kicks." Anyone else would have shut me up, but Hootie just laughed. I was in his arms in the bed he shared with his wife, and he laughed like we were two buddies sharing a joke.

"Fair enough," he said, which surprised me. Hootie isn't necessarily the philanthropic type, but I didn't question him. I deemed it had to be fate for it to be just that easy.

And it was a good thing, too, because I had been wanting to buy Wren a bike.

I drive back to Junction, stashing Hootie's dirty cash from my most recent visit in the glove compartment. It's a little after three now, and I always make sure to get in somewhere around five-thirty. My friend, Emmy, covers for me if Wren or Jerry ever drop by, but to my knowledge, they never have since picking up my afternoon "shift."

In the meantime, I go to the library there and get lost in a sea of books. I've never been a big reader before but have the luxury now, if you can spin it that way.

I read a lot of fiction, stories about women who make it out of a dark hole they've dug for themselves. No accident there, I suppose. And I lose myself in words and plot lines, trying not to think about the hard things I have to do like tell my boss I'm pregnant. And tell Wren I've failed again.

Sometimes, I think of my mother. How she was given the gift of closing the curtain before the show ever really began.

Lucky dog.

Chapter Twenty-Eight
Rochelle

I always wanted to get us a dog, but Glenn claims he's allergic. I just don't think he likes the idea of dog hair. So shamefully, I'll admit, when I see Kimber scamper along the marble floor in the foyer or bound up the stairs like a blonde collie, I close my eyes for a second and just pretend she's the newest addition to our family of two.

But then reality hits, and I see her touch Glenn's arm or drink orange juice out of a glass and the whole notion is popped, my little balloon. I'm back to being a middle-aged woman ravaged with cancer, living with her husband's mistress.

And I don't even have my own soap opera.

I spend my days reading the Bible. I make it very apparent I'm reading the Bible, when really, I'm not always even reading it. I'm trying to see a flicker of something in Kimber because my life depends on it. My current one anyways. I need to prove Glenn and Ann wrong.

And even though they haven't said it, I know what it looks like. The crazy sick lady living with her ex in a house of disgrace. I can change things. I have to change things like it's the last breath I take before going under. Otherwise, what have I done?

"You were like, alive in the fifties right? That's so cool." I've found myself outside on the patio during one of Texarkana's heat blankets of an evening. We're drinking something horribly sweet that tastes like a can of peaches went bad and somebody poured a bottle of vodka into it. But Kimber's relaxed and has her naked feet on the patio table. The same table where Glenn and I used to eat breakfast.

"It was the coolest," I say, ignoring the way it feels like my gums are rotting. Kimber's long legs are as naked as her feet, her shorts ending at her upper thigh. She's wearing a Mexican peasant top and bare shoulders. Her hair is sun-kissed and skin caramel from the sun. Glenn's tastes have evolved, apparently.

"And you guys had a son, right?" I don't take offense at Kimber's broken train of thought. And even though it would be kind to blame the candied vodka, I'm better in tune than that. Kimber is horribly more vapid than I even realized at first glance. It's another demon I'm fighting. Can you break through to someone who has no real understanding of what exists outside their skin, regardless of how unmarred that skin is?

"I had a son. Glenn had...a stepson." I want to say "a problem" but why dig up what's done? I haven't spoken about Mack for a long time to anyone other than Dr. Neese or my church group. I almost feel an urge to talk about him now, get all the words out before I'm shut back up. I pull my sweater around me. It's hotter than Hades but there's a constant chill inside me I try to ignore. I worry Glenn will walk by and see us, his beautiful girlfriend with his aging wife clad in a black matronly sweater in the middle of June.

"What about you? What was it like growing up?" I bite my cheek to keep from smirking. Kimber is still smack dab in the middle of the process. Kimber swallows down her peach slush, stretches out her long beautiful toes. I get the sudden urge to light up a Virginia Slim, a nasty habit I quit years ago.

"It wasn't a fairy tale. I mean, my mama tried to make it that way. She liked the way things looked. Actually, she liked what people thought about the way things looked. We were always dressed nicely. Always went to church. Always had a lot of friends, and she'd even invite her own over. Daddy would grill. I remember that smell. Seared meat." Kimber puckers her lips at another peachy swallow. I can smell it, too. Flesh on fire.

"But the nighttime was hard. And no, I don't want to talk about it." I can see Glenn flickering at the edge of my eye. He's inside the kitchen, a helpless fish in the aquarium beyond the sliding glass patio doors.

"Nighttime's always hard. For the best of us," I say, throwing out the rope and hoping she'll take it. But she doesn't.

"Glenn's the best thing that's ever happened to me." The moment's lost but another one comes at me. One where I'm sitting on my bed and Mack is asleep next to me. I'm sitting in my pajamas, and Dennis is leering at me from his shadowy spot in the doorway. And I say the same thing at him with my eyes on my lap. Like it's a dirty confession. And I'm hopelessly sorry for it.

"I know what that's like." It's the wrong thing to say because even though I'm lazily lobbing it over the net, she looks at me like I'm pointing a gun at her forehead. It always tickles me, this side of women: young, old, stupid, smart, sophisticated, barefoot and pregnant–we all take to that sharp edge when something's on the line. I call it "The Eve Effect."

"I know you do. But sometimes, things get a little stale. And it's not fair to that man in there. To have to sacrifice year over year and then wake up one day to realize the gift he's been given's gone rotten." The slap is as hard as it is invisible.

"So cancer's my fault? What it's done to me–that's my fault?"

"I wasn't talking about your body, Rochelle," she says. "I was talking about your heart." She takes her drink, steadies herself on two unsteady legs. I'm left to watch her walk away, using the full force of her arms to slide back the patio door. When she meets Glenn in the kitchen, she puts her drink down on the island, and she gives every inch of herself to him. I turn my eyes away.

I start to sweat beneath my sweater.

Chapter Twenty-Nine
Wren

I took the rest of my supply when Rhonda dropped me off, strong inhalations of forgetting. It was the best kind of feeling, that initial high. Like my brain wanted nothing to do with me, which was perfectly fine.

I walked outside for a while, not even feeling the cold. I walked behind the apartment complex, pastel-colored walls on one side, drainage ditch on the other. I likened walking to forgetting and kept going faster until my legs gave out and stumbled back up the stairs to the apartment.

Dad didn't even bother to show up.

Finally, Mom comes home. She says Jerry will be late, the Ballbarians wreaking major havoc on White Smoke's local bowling scene. I find pork rinds in the pantry and stuff my mouth, trying to sober up while Mom is in the shower. I drink down the rest of the Kool-Aid Jerry's made and try to list reasons why we can't leave. I need stability. I'm a kid for crying out loud and can't be jostled around like old furniture. If we keep moving, I'll probably end up being one of those kids who smacks everyone around.

I think about The Mule.

One thing at a time. I stuff more pork rinds in my mouth.

I hear Mom finishing up in the bathroom and the nausea is on me. I should be in bed, sleeping off the haze.

When she finally comes in, I'm sitting at the table. It's hard to keep a steady gaze on her, so I look at my hands, will my stomach to shut up.

"So. We need to talk."

"Yes," I say. The word is dry in my mouth, and I wish I could stand to get a cup of water.

"I don't even know how to begin."

"Let's just go with how you always do." I sigh it out, and I can feel Mom watching me.

"Wren, everything okay?"

"Still sick. Like yesterday."

"Oh, geez. You're not pregnant are you?" Mom raises a hand near my cheek. She's still standing, and I wish she'd sit. She's in her robe, no makeup. I wish the guys at Double Dees could get a glimpse of her, the notorious Natalie Reynolds, looking all of thirty-seven years right now. Maybe they'd actually see her as a human being for once.

"No, gah—no!"

"Okay, stomach bug then. Need to lie down?"

"No. Just tell me what you want to say." Finally, she sits in front of me, and it's just the two of us at the little brown table with the grandma chairs Jerry's mother gave him. The fridge is behind my back, and I concentrate on its deep hum so I don't throw up.

"Look, Jerry's a wonderful guy, and I'm happy we found him." If I didn't feel so horrible, I'd spit out a laugh. Treasure hunters, the two of us. Digging around for the shiniest meal ticket. "He loves me, I know that." Mom forks her fingers through her wet hair and stares up at a water stain on the ceiling. I wait to hear the feeling's mutual although I know it will never happen.

"Well, what then? Get out my suitcase, right?" Mom knits her eyebrows. Her lips pucker.

"Wren, I think you need to lie down."

"Just tell me!" I mean to slam my fist on the table, but I'm too soft with it. Mom's still staring at me.

"Wren, I'm pregnant." The processing takes a second too long. The refrigerator hums in and out of my thoughts and my belly is screaming at her. Pregnant. A brother. A sister. Someone else to shoulder this load. I think I feel something bloom beneath my strong desire to upchuck. Happiness.

"I wanted to tell you yesterday..."

"Oh, wow! Uh, I...I didn't know. That's so great, Mom!" I hope my face is smiling. My eyes burn with tears because it feels like what life is supposed to be, an unending circle.

Not a dead end.

"Look, Wren..."

"Do you know if it's a boy or girl? Wait, it's too early right? What about names? I've always liked–"

"I'm not keeping it, hun." Mom's back on the water stain, having a silent conversation with it above my head. The circle is snipped, and I'm back on my straight line to nowhere.

"Why? Jerry will be heartbroken."

"Jerry doesn't know and I–*we*–aren't going to tell him." Mom's eyes climb back down from the ceiling and are fierce in her head. I understand now. I don't want to place blame, but I figure it's always been there, hiding most likely behind my spleen. I finger it now, throw it at my mother.

"You would. You would ruin everything." I feel a burp of pork rinds and Kool-aid in my throat. I swallow hard. "I didn't want to move, you know. I wanted to stay close to him."

"He was gone, Wren. He wasn't there anymore, and we didn't have anyone to help us." Mimi, Aunt Rebecca, Abuelo, but I never bring them up because it always shuts her down.

"And we do now? Or do we just have some dude willing to deal with you as long as you sleep with him?" The shot's fired across the table and hits Mom in the heart. She starts nodding her head which scares me a little.

"Easy. Right? Right. Because..." Mom looks up again, catching her tears in her lids to keep them from falling. "Because it's just so dang easy to lose your whole world and then to raise your child after what she's seen. And you don't know how hard I loved that man. That stupid, selfish man." She wipes semi-circles under her eyes. "And it got me nowhere, Wren. That's where we are right now. That's our address.

Nowheresville. All I try to do is make sure you're fed and cared for, the best I can. My only goal. If you think any of this has anything to do with me, think again. And you know what? I messed up this time. I really don't even know how this happened, but it happened. And I have to live with the consequences. But you're going to have to forgive me."

"I don't have to do anything." The storm in my stomach calms. The refrigerator calms down, too. "I keep loving you and loving you. And I sometimes think, if I love you hard enough, it will be the right amount of love and something will happen. Maybe he will come back. Maybe we'll finally be better off. I don't know. But I've been wrong about that."

I get brave, look at Mom's face. My whole world smashed to pieces.

"Maybe I don't love you like I thought." It's a lie but I say it anyways. Eye for an eye. I think of Mrs. Ling but then shut the woman up in the refrigerator.

"Fair enough." Mom stands, clutches her robe. "But I'll never stop loving you, Wren. And I hope one day you'll understand all of this a little bit better."

I laugh on the inside again. There's no use understanding anything. I can hear Mrs. Ling pounding on the inside of the refrigerator door, and I try my best to ignore her. I look up and the water stain is growing larger like it's trying to devour the kitchen. The room spins, and I let it spin. Things are feeling dark but before the lights turn all the way off, I vomit all over Jerry's mother's kitchen table.

Again, I laugh.

Chapter Thirty
Natalie

Taking a shower only helped in that it was something to do. My skin still crawled afterwards, my head still filled with the sensory details of being with a man like Hootie.

A married man.

And it doesn't help that this time, my daughter waited for me to talk, and the conversation revolved around what I've done. And how I've ruined everyone's life.

The father isn't even the guy I live with.

How my life took a Jerry Springer turn, I'll never know. I've reworked it in my head so many ways, I can't figure it out. I feel like Rain Man, muttering to myself as all the possible possibilities run across the movie screen in my mind, just out of reach.

It went poorly, if you were wondering. So much so, my baby girl vomited all over the kitchen table. I didn't tell her the other, seedier side of all this. Sometimes, I think if I squeeze my eyes real tight and breathe real deep, I can make Hootie and his dirty cash go away.

But he's still there and so is the money I deposited in my bank account on the way home.

Fifty bucks for a spin with Miss Natalie.

I start to feel a little nauseous again, but this time it's not the pregnancy.

I don't let it run me over though because Wren is still sick. Sunday morning, and I let the sun run through the vertical blinds behind the couch. I sit with a cup of instant coffee in my hands that Jerry made for me before heading to church.

Our schtick: "You're shacking up with Jezebel, Jerry. You're likely to burst into flames the moment you walk into the door."

"Why do you think I need Jesus?" he says and smiles, smelling faintly of his Polo knock-off. He asked me once and only once if I wanted to go with him. I'm sure the ice in my eyes—and my veins for that matter—was enough to shut down that particular line of questioning.

My Jesus is this couch, the one Mack used to sit on with me, and the sun warming my back on such a frigid day. My daughter is still in bed and will probably be there until it's time to go to sleep again. She doesn't have a virus or a stomach bug. She's coming off something. Not sure what yet, but I'm sure that little punk Mareck has something to do with it. I'll take her to the doctor if she can't keep anything down later on. But I'd rather not have to do that.

The less paperwork documenting my stellar job of a mother, the better.

The foolishness of man perverteth his way: and his heart fretteth against the Lord.

It hits me like it sometimes does. The words of my father. It's never in his voice, more like a feeling masquerading as words.

I try to push it away but it only gets louder in my chest. I go and dump out the coffee, watch it run down the drain.

"What. Do. You. Want. Me. To. Do." I ask but not sure who. My friend, Emmy, would say "the universe." I think that's the biggest crock I've ever heard in my life, even more than the Jesus thing. When she says things like that, I ask her if I can borrow her foil helmet. Looking down the drain, I know it's not the universe, the mute creation that's spinning on its head like I feel I'm doing right now.

The foolishness of man perverteth his way...

I know. So shut up.

No, whatever is going on is something different. It's the eyes that watch me, the feeling that talks at me. It was easier when vodka was involved. I could shut everything off like switching off a television set.

But sober? I feel the world throb inside me like the blood coursing through my veins.

"Mooooom....." It sounds like a zombie is lazily making its way towards me.

But I know it's just my drug-addicted daughter needing me in the midst of the mess I've made.

Chapter Thirty-One
Rochelle

I go to the doctor. I play "guess what" and tell him all about Kimber, my living situation. Dr. Cohen is one of my most favorite people on the planet. I've known him since our primary physician recommended him the first time breast cancer decided to ravage my body. Even though I avoided treatment for over a year that last go round, he still talks to me. He's a gentleman like that.

He's also small, Jewish, on the skinnier side with thinning hair and glasses on the slight bump of his nose. He's younger than me, a strong forty, maybe. When I talk to him, I feel like I'm talking to Job, a man who had everything and lost it, but God's blessed him again. Dr. Cohen's first family died in a car he wasn't sitting in. He was at work, and his wife and two kids were coming home from school. And the first time he met me, he said it just like that. Factually. I suppose he wanted to clear up why he had two photos of himself with two very different families on his desk. The before and after.

I guess he wanted me to know that I didn't have the monopoly on misery.

"I can't imagine that's been going well," he says. His voice is as steady as his hands. His new wife looks taller than the older one, a bit more filled out. Substantial. I wonder if that was on purpose.

"You imagine correctly." I've been avoiding both of them, Kimber and Glenn. I wake up early, even earlier than Glenn who meets the sun every morning on his daily run. I make a frantic egg white and spinach scramble and eat it in my bed. I listen for footsteps to determine when I can leave my prison cell.

It's awful.

"Why did you agree to this arrangement?"

"That's funny. You make it sound like it's something that happened to me. Really, I almost requested it."

"Is that so?" I can tell Dr. Cohen is intrigued. He told me once that he writes short stories in his spare time. I wonder how he'll describe my aging face and hands. A vain thought but I don't know how to reel it back in.

"I wanted to fix it. Her, I guess. He's a lost cause," I say, counting the sunspots dancing across my knuckles. "Maybe I shouldn't think that way. I'm sure you're aware I'm supposed to share the Gospel."

"Oh, I'm aware," he says, not condescendingly but respectfully, like he too knows what it's like to hold somebody's soul in his hands.

"I feel like a failure. I wanted to get to know her and change her mind, not for my sake but for hers. For Glenn's. They're the type of people that live on a merry-go-round. I was that type of person too. But now I want off."

"And you're disappointed they won't follow you?" It gut punches me because it's true. Here we are trying to map out the best course of action for the stage I cancer inside of my nonexistent breast, and instead, Dr. Cohen is stating the obvious I've been shoving hard in the back closet of my mind.

Selfishly, I'm just pissed off about the whole thing.

"I mean, maybe on some level. It's not easy you know. People look at you like you're a freak when you start following Jesus. You're totally different than you used to be, and somehow, this is an evil thing. And I know why. It makes them consider that maybe they don't have it all figured out. That maybe I'm onto something. Or maybe they're just scared that I'll drag them along into a life of sobriety and knee pain from all the praying." It wasn't hard to determine which camp Glenn was in. "But that's not it at all. I'm just trying to show them the danger in believing in yourself and yourself alone. It's a house of cards."

Dr. Cohen nods his head, sandwiched between his two families. "'If anyone will not welcome you or listen to your words, leave that home or town and shake the dust off your feet.' I believe that's in Matthew."

"You know the New Testament?"

"I'm somewhat familiar. I enjoy reading. A lot. And I think your Jesus was fairly wise." It stabs at my heart to hear the "your." I want to replace it with "our" because that's the only way to look at Christ. But I think of what Dr. Cohen just said.

"It's time to dust off my feet?"

"In this case, I'd say it's long overdue."

Chapter Thirty-Two
Wren

I woke up Sunday, late afternoon, with a horrendous headache and Mom's face bobbing above me. We didn't speak, but I could feel Mom's hand feeling my forehead and holding my hand. I fell asleep again, and now it's early Monday morning when I wake. Fresher this time. Ready to face the day even if what's left of my heart keeps rattling in my chest.

Then I remember The Mule.

I think about skipping but figure it's pointless. I'm going to die at some point, might as well be today.

On that note, I find Jerry packing his lunch in the kitchen and ask him for a ride. We leave the apartment together, and I feel like the sidekick to an incredibly bubbly super hero.

"You know, this is kind of fun, Wrennifer. You can always hitch a ride with me. Just figured you were still going to school with that Marcus kid."

"Mareck."

"Yep, that's the one." I look at Jerry bopping in his seat to the Temptations. Poor, sweet Jerry. There's a tiny spark of anger that's coiled deep in my heart. I lit it when I avoided Mom in the kitchen this morning, and I watch it burn as I think of Mom's hand on my forehead, pretending everything's okay.

I want the blaze to run so rampant that I consider telling Jerry about his unborn kid. But instead, I just watch the show, Jerry snapping his fingers and bobbing his head and somehow directing us through early White Smoke traffic without leaving a trail of bodies in his wake.

For the first time in my life, I'm early for school. I jump out of the A/C van as fast as I can and wave at Jerry like I'm waving off an unknown attacker. I keep my eyes down and hands shoved into my coat pockets but nobody's staring at me because at this hour, it's just a bunch of nerds walking in with me doing the same exact thing.

In the office next to Zinberg's, I go in and ask the secretary for my backpack. It's retrieved and still wet from languishing in the yard for who knows how long. I take it to the bathroom and dry it out under one of the driers then hurry to my locker so I won't have to see Mareck.

Too late.

"Miss America," he says, but he sounds different. I'm almost worried about him since we still have five minutes until the late bell rings.

"You're early."

"I found a ride," he says.

"What'd you do? Sell my bike for parts?"

"Keep cool. It's at the trailer. I take it you're still livid?" I'm thrown off by the question, not by the words but how Mareck asks it. It's the eyes I realize, dead and stony in his face. There's no light, no teasing. I could probably tell him I have a machete in my bag with his name on it, and he wouldn't even smirk.

"What happened to you?" I ask. I forget myself and touch his arm, but he moves away. He grabs his books from the locker and says, "Ah, nothing. Just finally got around to doing something I should have a long time ago."

He slams the locker door in my face, and he strolls down the hall, grabs The Redhead's waist when he meets up with her. I try to process what's happened but that's like eating a mouthful of rocks. So I reopen the locker. Take my books. And pray Leslie Buell finishes me off.

Chapter Thirty-Three
Natalie

It's a Monday. It's not the best day to confront Hootie.

So I do it anyways.

His wife is what you would call "petite," that section in the clothing department reserved for underfed librarians. She's very anti-Hootie. Whereas Hootie looks like an overgrown mountain man with a big personality, Denise is slight and blonde, her hair in a perfect bob. She's the perfect soccer mom who can afford to roll around in a Honda Odyssey and whose nails are the perfect shade of Passion Pink.

My nails look like they've been through a meat grinder.

That's what I'm doing, looking at my nail beds, at my weathered hands, parked out front of Hootie's condo as frank as day. I could have cornered him in his office but there are too many wandering ears about that place. And then there's the real reason I'm here: I want the threat to be real. I could tell his wife at any point he doesn't cooperate.

I make the mistake of looking in the rearview mirror. I see gunk in my right eye, and then I start to tear up. I'm a mess. I feel a mess. I'm about to take a man's whole world and dangle it above his head.

I think of Mack's dangling feet, and my eyes burn when I shut them.

If only it had gone better with Wren. She didn't make it easy. She must have been high to think she, Jerry, and I would make the perfect little family. I didn't have the heart to tell her there's no way this is Jerry's baby. The man won't sleep with me. He's too much of a gentleman that way. Mostly, I hold him while he cries in the dark, unraveling and re-braiding the sick things his mother did to him as a child.

Yes, I see the pattern. Yes, I have a problem.

But other than a long gone Dr. Carol, I've got no one to spill this to.

I can see her in the front window, Denise. There must be a piano or a desk against the window facing the street because she leans over one of her children, points at something in front of them.

Oh heck, I think, smacking open the glove compartment and spritzing frenziedly at my face and hair. Might as well talk to the real boss of the family.

Lord knows, Hootie isn't man enough to wear that hat.

Chapter Thirty-Four
Rochelle

"No one would blame you, Ro. For trying." Ann sits on my bed in a silk leopard print tank top. She has a matching headband in her hair, ankles crossed, and I'm taking a snapshot of her in my mind. I'm going to miss her way too much.

"Trying what, though? I was thinking about it, Ann. What Dr. Cohen said. What he didn't even have to say. I was trying to make amends for the person I used to be." I think of that girl, all versions of her. The knobby-kneed child who tied up her brother and then the teenager in her short shorts and bubblegum lip gloss. The young woman almost left for dead in somebody's yard and then the one who became a mother and couldn't really manage that gig. I think of the one right now, who closes the eyes inside her mind and says an "I'm sorry" to God.

The one without her breasts but a heart still beating.

"If you go, I might not see you again." Now it's Ann's turn to play Dr. Cohen's part. Factual. I scoot her over with my hip and sit leg to leg with her. I hold her while she cries even though I'm the one who wants to. It's not a matter of "might." I already feel in my bones that this is my final act.

"I'll call you. I'll write. I'll let you know if this all turns out to be one big ol' mess."

"It won't be, Ro. God's guiding you on this one, not yourself. You know it's what you have to do." I nod. It is. Mack is a baby again in my arms. All that dark, dark hair. In my head, I hold him to the breast I still have. Can you imagine living with a psychotic brother and no other family to love you? I don't even have to imagine it. Because it was life. Another something I give to God because it's too heavy to hold onto.

I'm sorry, Mack. Because I was just a child, too. And that's a hard thing for anyone to understand.

Ann tells me she loves me, and we talk some more over cups of coffee I've stealthily commandeered from the kitchen. But I don't have to worry because Glenn and Kimber have gone to who knows where.

She leaves eventually, and I'm left on my bed in one of our–Glenn's– absurdly large guest rooms. My suitcase is packed, and there are a couple of small boxes I picked up from Wal-Mart that I've filled with my books, my hair dryer. It's almost shocking what little is actually mine in this house and how little I actually want.

I tiptoe down the stairs, ears straining for sounds of movement. But the inside of Glenn's home is dead, except for me. I walk to the library to look out the window. I stand at it and stare at the tree, trying to kick start my mind to remember. Wren. She was so little then, just a small girl at her father's funeral. And then I remember when she was a little bigger, holding my hand when we'd go to church together. Natalie thinks I ruined her. I don't imagine I did. At least that wasn't the intent. I just wanted Wren to know who she could trust when she couldn't trust anyone.

Because that day always seems to come.

I wonder how she is now. If she's a bigger version of that same sweet little girl. I stopped receiving photos a while ago. But I never stopped writing to her even when I stopped hearing back. "They probably moved," Ann had said to me once. Which only served to fatten the worried worm in my stomach.

"What do you see when you stare out of it?" For a second, it's all the times before this one, and I'm waiting for Glenn to wrap his arms around me. But he hovers instead near my right shoulder looking out the same window. I can feel him, smell his warmth and something new on his clothes. Chinese.

"How were the potstickers?"

"Delightful as usual. I would have invited you along with us but since Ann..."

"No need. We had a good time," I say. I don't dissect his comment, the lie in it. Instead, I turn and face the prize I had coveted for so very long. And all I see is a man.

"I'm leaving," I say. I've been mulling this over and breaking it down so often for the past few weeks that it feels like tissue paper in my hand. After talking with Kimber, I realized something for the first time. I can't save anyone. I couldn't save Mack or Wren or a misguided young Kimber whose brain is saturated with the same lies that live in Glenn's heart.

Only Jesus can do something like that. I'm simply the messenger.

"Oh? Where will you go?" I have to muffle a little laugh. I've often wondered if Glenn views me as a doll, one that only breathes and moves in his presence. I wonder if he feels the same way about Kimber.

"White Smoke," I say. It's plain as a day to me. God made it that way. I've been having dreams, praying prayers. I keep seeing it, the apartment, the time I spent with Wren while Natalie got her life together. I don't even know where they are now. But I know God will help me find them.

"I'll give you money." This is Glenn's way of loving me because I know now; he doesn't fully understand what love is. I've known that for a while, if I'm honest. I knew that the day I got baptized when Glenn wasn't next to me. When I was pondering the unfathomable gift of Christ trading His life for my own and how I couldn't even gather the courage to tell my husband about it.

How Glenn complained that I'd left the crust on his sandwich when I got home that day.

The divide was already a river wide and there was nothing I could do to stop it.

"Okay," I say when he takes me into his arms. My mouth muffles the word into his shoulder. I wish I could say I didn't need it and had a ton of money saved up in a shoe box under my bed. But honestly, I've felt this was part of the plan too. *Can you swallow down your pride just one last time to do My will?* Yes, Lord.

He pulls me back and peels me off of him. His strong hands are gripping my shoulders, and I try not to think of his hands on Kimber. Too late.

"We'll miss you, Rochelle." His eyes flicker, an eraser gliding over the first word. "*I'll* miss you."

"I know," I say and press my nose back into his shoulder. But he just doesn't smell the same way anymore.

• • • •

THE NEXT MORNING IS quick and uneventful. It's early, the way I want it. I'll be driving for a long time. Glenn and I barely discussed the details but a divorce is in order. He said he'll talk with me once I'm up there, and we'll work something out.

"Quick and painless." I had to stifle another laugh.

He lets me keep the Jaguar, a sick little parting gift. My whole life is inside that car, and as I drive away–Kimber with her messy bedhead, one arm raised and the other lazily around Glenn's waist–I imagine the flames licking the sides of the house and God bringing down what we had only pretended to build.

I can only hope in the next phase, there will be no pretending.

Chapter Thirty-Five
Wren

I'm so bothered by Mareck that I sizzle out The Mule's desire to clobber me.

She follows me with her eyes throughout the day. I feel like they're dressed up in her skirt and whale sweater, Big Louis somehow slung over an invisible shoulder, and we walk the halls together, drawing White Smoke babies in our heads.

And I'm not even high.

"You're a real killjoy, you know that?" We're in the basement bathroom, and it's just me and Leslie who finally corners me. I'm guessing she's on the outs with the cohorts because they're not here right now. Earlier, they were pressed shoulder to shoulder walking down the hall, The Mule nowhere to be found.

Her face looks like it's made enemies with a brick wall, and I swallow down the sick sense of pride in my throat.

"What does it matter what I am? Nothing matters anymore," I say. I press my back against the tiled wall, attempting to ignore the years of bacteria that has colonized there as I slide slowly down to the floor. When she followed me in here, I knew it was the end, and I was grateful for it. And I can only imagine she saw that, a sense of peace, and was too thrown off to punch it off my face.

"What are you talking about, loser?" Leslie slides down with me, giving me a better shot of her getup. She's wearing a different whale sweater this time and flared khakis instead of the tights and skirt she was wearing last week. She looks like she's working second shift at the GAP. I don't know how I feel about it, the fact that Leslie and I both look like somebody else dressed us.

"Mareck. He left me. He's hooked up with some red headed chick. One of yours, I think. If not, you need to hand her an application."

"That's what you're all sourpuss about? Mareck? The guy who thinks Tony the Tiger invented frosted flakes?" She's looking at me like I've grown extra heads. She puts Big Louis in her lap and excavates the inside with her hand. She delicately removes a tub of gloss she applies with her very thick pinkie.

"There's more to him than that." I don't go into detail. Mareck lives with his grandfather and brother in a trailer off a road in the woods that's not really a road. It feels like I'm going to be obliterated via chainsaw every time I'm out there, and his grandfather, Franklin, a drunk in a wifebeater, doesn't do anything to alleviate that feeling. But I go with Mareck because of what Mareck's told me. Because of the scars on Mareck's legs.

I'm not the only one dealing with a bully.

"People are more than the stupid stuff they say."

"Ah, how poetic. But are they more than the stupid stuff they are?" The Mule asks me, point blank. I imagine she's thinking of Wanda and that other one now. "Must suck when nobody's got your back. Oh wait."

"Why do you even need those two? I mean, I imagine they're good for the ego, but I think I'd lose my mind having to babysit every day."

"I don't *need* them like you don't *need* Mareck. It just doesn't blow having someone else to help shoulder the responsibility."

"Responsibility for what? Deciding who wears pink on Wednesdays?" For a moment, I think our little camaraderie has ended, and she's about to introduce her fist to my face, but she settles down.

"No, smart aleck. I've created an entire dynasty. This thing continues on with or without me, and you bet your backside I'm going nowhere until they cart me off the stage next year during graduation." She dunks her pinkie in again and if it weren't for the slick glob on it, I'm certain she'd set her lips on fire with her frantic rubbing. "That redhead? Her name's Miranda. She's a freshman looking to take my place. *My. Place.* Girl's lost it if she thinks she's any match for me." I have to agree with her, but something in Leslie's eyes makes her seem worried. Which oddly makes me worry. Not like Leslie Buell's my dream bully or anything, but at least she's comfortable. Like my favorite big-boned blanket.

"Miranda," I say. It sits like poison on my tongue. "Mareck was weird today."

"When is he not?" she says, wiping her saturated pinkie on her sweater. I cringe knowing if I owned that thing, I'd keep it covered in protective plastic.

"No, I mean he seemed like his soul's been sucked right out of him. He said he finally got around to doing something he's been meaning to for a long time now."

"Break up with you?"

"I hadn't considered that until just this moment."

"Sorry," she says, and I can tell she kind of means it.

"No. I think something happened. I wish he'd talk to me." The loneliness kicks in even though someone is sitting right next to me. It's the panic of being alone, something that always lingers at my shoulder. And now that Mareck's left, it's something that sits beneath my skin like a very concerning splinter. I wish I could talk to Mrs. Ling right now.

"I didn't do anything with him." Leslie stares at the wall in front of us. The bell for fifth period rings but neither of us moves.

"Really?"

"No. I just wanted to piss you off."

"Then why did he make me think you did?"

She turns and looks me in the face. "Because he's Mareck. He doesn't care about you, Wren. And I'm actually not saying that to hurt you. He's damaged goods. Damaged goods hurt and keep hurting," she says, turning to the wall again. I want to press her, but the second bell rings and detention doesn't seem appealing at the moment. Besides, I have my Cornerstone Club meeting and against all odds, I'm kind of looking forward to it.

Leslie rustles her bag, makes to leave. I feel like something important is ending, and I really don't want it to.

"What are you doing after school?" I ask.

Chapter Thirty-Six
Natalie

Denise smells good. Better than me. She's wearing real perfume, not some clearance special from the Piggly Wiggly. She naturally braces her chest with crossed arms and puckers her lips at me. *Look what the cat dragged in. One of Hootie's used up girls from the restaurant.*

"Can I help you?" I know she knows who I am. She came to one of our Christmas parties and looked like she didn't want to touch anything. I didn't blame her. She was wearing a wine colored knit sweater and black cigarette plants. Emmy was wearing a Santa bikini with mistletoe in her hair. She thinks we're cut from a very different cloth, but I desperately want to tell her I'm not like the rest of them. That this is just some game I got thrown into, and I'm just doing my best to learn how to win it.

She keeps me outside the door, on the edge of her reality. It reminds me of the time I approached Greg Zinberg about his drug-addled wife. Funny, how he's Wren's principal now. Fortunately, she seems to hate him as much as I do.

And fortunately, she has no idea how he's connected to my past.

"I was looking for Hootie." Where could that man be? He'll typically take off for lunch to spend "family time" with his homeschooling wife and two kids. But knowing him, that's probably some sort of front.

"He's not here. He's working." She looks at me quizzically like she's already caught on that he must be somewhere else then. Her face resurfaces, and she's made peace with the truth she already knows in her heart. Hootie's no good.

"Right. But look, I think I can talk with you instead." She stays firm against the threshold, bracing herself even tighter with her two arms. I think I can almost sense relief in her strained pose, like, *Give me what you've got. I've trained for this.*

"I'm pregnant. And I don't want to hurt you guys. But knowing Hootie, he'd work some way around this and never let you know. I don't know what I'm going to do. I might need help, and I can't do it alone...financially. Just know I'm sorry. I'm really very sorry. I mean that." I hear a small voice inside, a child calling from the back of the condo.

"One sec, Robbie," Denise says and turns back to me. She smiles like a snake that's just eaten a bird.

"You think I was born yesterday?" She unlocks her arms and takes a tiny step towards me. I try to find the edge of her front stoop behind me with my boot. "Hootie has all kinds of girls just like you. You're no different. You're not special. You're trash, straight from the trailer. But you know what? It works for us. He gives me a good home, the money I need to raise my kids, to get my hair done. And he gets to spend time on his sad little hobby." Her eyes seem to have a tough time swallowing down the "sad" part. "You don't scare me. And you're certainly not exploiting me. So you'll just have to decide to have that kid of yours and get a paternity test because until then, nobody's doing jack squat for you."

I finally find it, the edge behind me. I teeter for a second, bracing myself for when her hands are placed on my shoulders and she pushes me off. But she doesn't. She just smirks and shuts the door firmly in my face. And I realize I'm the one that has taken me to the edge. I'm the one waiting to fall.

Chapter Thirty-Seven
Rochelle

S even months. That's how long I've been waiting.

It took only a day to find a small rental in White Smoke with a landlord that's only slightly creepy. Glenn wires me the money monthly, and I call to confirm I received it. The machine always picks up.

I go to church. It's the same one I used to take Wren to, tucked away in a metal building in the woods; some of the people don't seem right. It's like they're part of the building, pieces to a set. No growth. No change. I've helped twice with the end of the month dinner and went to bingo once. Every time, I get hard stares, and I think it's because I wear lipstick. I feel Jesus on the edge, where the trees line the building, watching. What He'd have to say to these people.

I haven't gone back in two weeks.

I got a job. It's not much, but it fills my time and gives me a little extra spending money on top of what Glenn sends me. I'll have to find something more permanent once the divorce goes through. I've tried to bring it up, but I can hardly ever get Glenn on the phone, and when I did that once when I first got to White Smoke, he brushed it off, said it was "too premature."

"What do we need to wait for Glenn? Kimber got any sisters moving in?" I said it light-heartedly because that's the way I feel about it. It no longer eats my heart, but by the way Glenn answered with a guttural mumble, it sounds like it's still snacking on his.

It's at a Hallmark store, my job. I man the cash register which took a few days to get right. I stock the cards and dust the doo-dads they sell there. It's a mom and pop operation, Pop having been long dead for ten years now. But Mom's nice. Her name is Gladys and she looks like something that should be sold in the store. I glossed over my existence.

"My granddaughter lives nearby," is all I said when she asked why I moved from Texarkana. That was good enough for her, which is one of the reasons I like her so much.

I've spent my evenings trying to find them. I've scoured the phone book. I mention Natalie in passing to strangers who scrunch up their faces and shrug their shoulders. I spend too much time at the Piggly Wiggly that smells like a bag of pork rinds exploded and at a gas station called Floyd's where people seem to congregate regularly. But to no avail. Jesus, why did you bring me here?

I give up. I think about packing everything into my small suitcase and moving in with Ann and her husband, Marty, who only seems to exist in glimpses. He's not the kind of guy to care if a random woman starts living in his house. Kind of like Glenn, only less questionable.

I'm thinking these thoughts when the doorbell rings. The heater's gone out. Perfect. But at least Creepy Landlord Lester is on top of it. I have an uneasy feeling that if I said jump, he'd ask how high. I go to let the repair man in. When I open the door, he's wearing a bomber jacket over his uniform which consists of shorts. In February.

"Hi, I'm Jerry!" he says with a big smile on his face. He offers me his fleshy hand.

I'm not sure what it is, but there's something about this man I honestly like.

Chapter Thirty-Eight
Wren

When I bring Leslie with me, it's like bringing a lion to a gazelle party. I've never seen wider eyes. But Rhonda remains level-headed in the fact that she doesn't jump out the window when we walk in.

I try my best to pretend that some of the stares aren't aimed at me.

"Welcome," Rhonda says and drifts in front of the desk where a dozing Mr. Sokolov sits as the club's sponsor. "Before we begin, let's start talking about what we're thankful for." I almost choke on the spit in my throat. Thankful. That's a good one. *Well, I don't know Rhonda. Let's see, there's my mother's impending abortion. That one should be a real riot. My boyfriend left me for someone ten times prettier, and I'm sitting right next to the girl I knocked out the other day and who could very well jump me when nobody's looking. So...yeah, feeling fan-freaking-tastic!*

Fortunately, I don't go first. That honor goes to Melissa Tate who's more than happy to dive into her life's crowning achievements. Tate is the type that should be part of Leslie's crew except for her extreme love affair with Jesus. But she dresses the part anyways with her baggy jeans and tight Areopostale top. She's wearing some sort of funky boot that says "Ugg" on the back. As much as Leslie pretends to have money, Melissa Tate is the real deal. Maybe it pays to friend Jesus.

I instantly feel the stab of guilt. I remember Mimi. I remember how she feels about Jesus.

How I felt about him once too.

"I'm just...I'm just so emotional right now you guys," Melinda says, cupping her invisible emotions with her hands. "We found this dog this weekend just walking down our street. It had a collar, so we kept calling the number on it but no one would pick up. Like, why wouldn't you be worried about your dog? We left a message with our name and address though. And yesterday, the owners finally came to pick it up. They had been on a weekend vacay!" The last line is the clincher, and she's waiting for all of us to express our mutual relief and gratitude. I look over at Leslie who starts to slow clap. I have to bite the inside of my cheeks so I don't lose it.

"That's...great. That's great," Rhonda says, cherry picking her words. I'm starting to give her a lot more credit for running this looney bin. Her eyes roam the room, and I pray I instantly disappear or she forgets I exist. But she finds me, looks at me hard. A challenge.

"Wren. I know you're new here, but I also know you have something to be grateful for. We all do," she says, making it irrefutable. Fine. I can play that game.

"Oh gosh, well I don't know if I can top that dog story. Thank you for that, Melissa, by the way," I say in my sweetest "I could be a Christian too, I just don't wanna" voice. Leslie snickers at my right, and Melissa side-eyes me as if I'm a dropping left by the mutt she found.

"If I had to choose just one wonderful thing to be grateful for, I think it would be that we all get to die. Now hear me out," I say, jazzing my hands even though nobody's attempting to argue against my point. "It's just a relief to know that one day, this will all be over. We won't have to pretend to like anyone or that we're just the sweetest little bit of candy on the planet," I say, hooking Melissa's eye like a fish. "One day, we'll get to fly right out of here into the great unknown, and nobody's going to pretend to love us." I choke a little on the last part but recover. "So that, dear Rhonda, is what I'm currently grateful for." Mr. Sokolov snorts a little in his sleep, but other than that, a pin could drop. Until we all hear the painfully slow clap of Leslie's hands.

• • • •

WHEN WE LEAVE, RHONDA thanks us for coming. She's lined out our next group activity at Morningside on Saturday and has invited all of us to participate, much to Melissa Tate's very palpable chagrin.

As we leave, I almost feel the need to apologize. I can tell she's not mad, not angry. She's disappointed, like a worn out parent who's tired of always having to be the responsible one. It didn't help that Aleski Bjorkland, the foreign exchange student, said he was thankful for raw meat.

Out in the empty hall, Leslie and I walk to the double doors. I try not to make it a big deal in my head that the last time we were outside on school grounds we were intent on beating the living snot out of each other.

"What you said in there. I know you were joking but...were you serious?" She turns to me. She looks stale, her morning fresh lip gloss and blow-dried hair have both gone flat. I try to determine what she's really asking.

"No, Leslie," I say. "I don't want to kill myself."

"Okay," she says, and we continue walking. We pass Zinberg's office, and I get a little sadder knowing there's a really corny photo of Rhonda trapped in there.

"Because if you really did feel that way..."

"Drop it," I say. I come to my senses. "Sorry."

"Don't be. I can drop you off," she says, nodding at her white Cabriolet waiting for her in the student parking lot. It's tempting. I imagine myself becoming best friends with her and borrowing her clothes (which she of course has tailored for me) and replacing both horse face and that other one because one of me is worth two of them. But I know Rhonda's still inside. I need to make things right.

"Thanks, but there's actually something I forgot to do. But Leslie, I'm sorry about–" I make a lazy circle around my face, and she nods.

"Don't sweat it. I deserved it." She's still staring at her car, but I can tell she can no longer see it. "You ever just over everything?" I look at her again and see something the same, yet different. Her tired face and hair and the too big bag weighing her down. It makes me wonder how she'd really dress herself, given the chance.

"Yeah. I really really am," I say without an ounce of lie in it.

"Oh good. I'm not the only one then." She smiles, the deeply pink side of her face shining in the sun. My fist instinctively aches.

"Leslie?"

"Yeah?"

"Uh, maybe tomorrow? Lunch? You think we'd give the entire student body a myocardial infarction if we sat together?"

"Oh, we definitely would. So yeah, let's do that." She smiles and walks away.

I wait a beat in the cold, in the sun before going back inside, getting used to the words I normally don't say, let alone hear: I'm sorry.

Chapter Thirty-Nine
Natalie

The air, the cold. I can't feel them anymore. *It was a mistake*, I think, working my way down Denise's front walkway. The lingering bit of nausea in my belly multiplies, and I upchuck my small lunch of saltines and deli ham into the planter next to Denise's brick mailbox. When I look up, she's no longer in the window and neither is the child I'm assuming is Ronnie.

I shouldn't have come. There was no reason to tell her any of that. I wasn't clearing the air. I wasn't doing the womanly thing and owning up to my actions. I was trying to hurt a woman I've always wanted to be.

But never will.

Women like that just don't get it. They think it's easy. They just fall into marriage, have the kids and bingo bango, life's a dream. I'm ignoring the fact that Denise's husband is a sleeze who entertains women in their own bed when Denise isn't around. But she's aware of the arrangement. Perhaps, she's even the brains behind it. Wouldn't surprise me with a woman like that.

I think about Mack. I couldn't have let him do that, not just to me, not just to Wren but to himself. I know, I know. I'm no fun. Why wouldn't a good romp in the hay only serve to strengthen a man? But if there's only one thing I know, it's hearts. How they lay bare, even when you attempt to seal them up. And Mack's heart was messy. It couldn't bear the weight of another one shouldering it's way in, attempting to play house, even if only for a night.

Someone like Hootie? It's different, maybe. Duplicitous, that's the word. He's one way with Denise, another way with all us–*cringe*–women. And that scares me. This little world I've planted two feet in, not only mine, but Wren's, too. How you can find someone who keeps one eye on you but one eye somewhere else, and how it only makes me angry because I envy being able to look away.

Here's what will happen: nothing. Denise won't say a word to Hootie. I won't either. I need the money for the abortion, so I'll have to get it another way. Tell Jerry I want to enroll into art school, how it's always been my dream. Bring home scraps of macaroni glued to styrofoam plates I hastily craft in my car.

I don't know. All I know is that Wren's eyes are working the same way. One on me, one somewhere else. And if I'm not careful, I'll lose both for good.

Chapter Forty
Rochelle

Jerry is a curious creature. He doesn't remind me of a typical man, and that's truly not a knock on him. I suppose I don't have much to compare him to other than my father, Glenn, Dennis, Mack. The last one who had my heart but still blew away like the wind. Jerry seems more substantial. His weight keeps him anchored, and he seems like one of those people who are thoroughly themselves and have no qualms about it.

"Righty-o. Let's take a looksie-loo at that little heat pump of yours." See.

I direct him out the back through the sliding glass windows. The yard is small and mushy, and he presses his weight into each step. *Talk to him.* I hear it in my breastbone. This man who has a thick head of hair like a helmet and a nature as intimidating as a titmouse.

Talk to him. Okay, I say, and go to make another carafe of coffee.

I've put the heat up a degree, and when he comes in, he politely wipes his boots on the rug. He reminds me of a snowman melting off a layer.

"Come, sit," I say in a way that's authoritative. It feels like there's a stranger in my chest.

"Oh, no I couldn't. I have more houses."

"Please. Just for a moment." I know he's sandwiched between his sense of duty and his sense of keeping the peace. We're not too different, Jerry and I. I pour him a coffee–black–and add a splash to my already lukewarm cup.

"I'm new," I say. I want to giggle as I watch his face process what I've just said. "To White Smoke."

"Oh, is that right? Where'd you come from?"

"Texarkana."

"Oh wow! That's brave."

"Is it?"

"Yeah. I mean traveling all that way. I've never been anywhere but White Smoke." He says it sincerely followed by a tentative sip from his cup. I believe him. Thoroughly.

"It was brave, I guess. Couldn't have gotten here without God," I say. I wait for it, the eye roll. But he nods his head so fast, his slicked back hair flashes light at me.

"Oh, no, I understand that. Take the woman I'm living with. I prayed for her." He talks to his coffee cup. His voice is soft and gentle like he's talking to a kitten.

"Is she everything you prayed for?" He reminds me of me. I remember laying face planted to the ceiling, praying that someone like Glenn would come along and take the misery away. The misery of being a single mother. The misery of living with my brother. I thought someone like Glenn could solve everything.

And now, everything's even more of a puzzle than it was back then.

He looks at his kitten cup for a moment, strokes the side with his thick hand. "No." One word. A hard drop in the bucket.

"It's at least admirable you're honest about that. I haven't been honest in thirty years." I smile, but I see his face. He's crying.

He wipes his eyes with his fingers. "She's pregnant. She's going to leave me."

"She doesn't want to raise your child with you?"

"It's not mine. I...we don't do that. I have my reasons," he says, a rehearsed line, I'm sure.

"No, I get that. People care too much about...that. Keeps them distracted about what's really happening around them." And boy, do I know that one from experience.

"Oh, Natalie. She's my queen." I perk up at the name. But no, could it? Natalie is, well, a beauty. And not to knock on poor Jerry. He seems like a quality guy but certainly not the type to handle someone like that.

"You know, I met a Natalie the other day," I fib. "Is her last name Reynolds?" I say, turning my own cup into a kitten and holding onto it with my eyes.

"Yeah, you know her?"

"Yes," I say in a short breath. "Where do you guys live? I was actually thinking of getting in touch with her again. She seemed really sweet."

"Over at the Legends Apartments. You know, that might do her some good. Get some advice from someone like you. Someone who has her head on her shoulders."

I nearly drop my cup but firm my hold on it. "Well, I suppose age wisens a person. Well, God, really."

"Ain't that the truth. Natalie doesn't believe in God. She says I'm wasting my energy." His voice goes soft again, and I feel the urge to wrap him in a hug.

"Some people don't. Until they do."

"Yeah, I guess you're right about that." He stares off at something behind my head. "She doesn't know I know. She's been getting nauseous, pale. I looked through her purse. I know I shouldn't have but she had some trouble with...well, alcohol, a long time ago, and I was afraid she fell off the wagon again. But instead of finding booze, I found a pregnancy test."

"Wow," leaves my mouth in a tiny puff of breath.

Jerry comes to life again when he glances down at the cup in his hands. "Thanks for the coffee. I really do need to get going." I scramble up with him, not wanting this moment to be quite over.

"Sure, sure. Um, what number again at The Legends? I'll see if I can make it there this weekend." After I stalk around in my car tonight.

"Thirteen. Lucky number," he rolls his sharp green eyes and snorts. "Seriously, that would be great if you'd talk with her. I know she did a horrible thing. But I love her. I forgive her. I need her to know that. I think it would be really great if you spent some time with her."

I still my heart with the imaginary pair of hands in my chest. "Me, too."

Chapter Forty-One
Wren

"I thought she was going to eat us."

"You? Miss 'I'm not afraid of anything.' *You* were afraid of little ol' Leslie Buell?" I say.

"I think you may be exaggerating on the 'little.'" Rhonda and I are sitting in the girls' locker room, backs against wall. Her Dad, I mean Zinberg, had to finish up some paperwork which gave us time to roam. I invited her because lunch here has been lonely without Mareck.

"She doesn't like herself. She doesn't like that she's a part of The Preps. She seems...tired."

"Not surprising. It must take a lot of energy balancing on top of all those bodies," Rhonda says. I think of a human pyramid, Leslie shifting her weight on the very top. Her metallic ballet flat grinding into the The Redhead's crown.

I feel a little guilty.

I swallow hard and look at Rhonda. Rhonda with her cotton candy hair and pilled black sweatpants. She seems unmovable even though I'm sure far too many people have taken a stab at it. I can relate.

"You know what you said about Mrs. Ling. How she changed your life? What did you mean by that?" It smells like a sad attempt at showering off sweat in here. There's a faint chemical scent beneath the body odor and the hormonal stench of fear. I don't look Rhonda in the eye. I can already feel it burning inside me, what she's going to say.

"Her faith. Her faith in something unseen, something I used to think was so so stupid. I'm not a God person. I'm a facts person, a reason person." Rhonda sits criss-cross, her right leg bobbing in time. "But she is, too. I don't know. She seems almost ethereal in the way she approaches life. And I felt so...base in comparison."

"What changed?"

"Me. I was the roadblock. I had to get over myself. If I was ever going to believe something next level, I had to die to myself."

"I have to imagine that was no picnic." My legs are stretched out, crossed at the ankles, like they always were with Mareck next to my hip.

"What in life is?"

Chapter Forty-Two
Natalie

I skip through the days, avoiding the cracks. I wake up early. I leave early. Earlier than both of them. When Jerry reaches for me at night, I'm not there. I'm on the couch curled up like a child. At work, there's a grim smirk on Hootie's, face but he doesn't look at me. He doesn't call me in to fire me either. He certainly doesn't ask to see me at the condo again. I guess he wants to keep things status quo and not spark some sort of scandal. And that's fine.

Just fine.

I don't mean to do it, but I do anyway. I go to the liquor store in Junction after my early evening lunch at TGI Fridays. It's the first Saturday in a long while that I don't need to go waste time there anymore, but I feel like I need a friend. So first, I go and see the waitress.

She brings me my broccoli cheddar soup and then slides into the booth. It's slow this time of day, plus her manager, Dave, had a doctor's appointment.

"Double Dee's. I've driven by that place before. What's that like?"

"A barrel of kittens," I say in between bites. I study the buttons on her vest, her name tag that spells Tiffany with an "ie" on the end. She has freckle-ly hands and there's a puff of red bangs at the top of her head. I get the urge to tell her her name doesn't make sense. But I don't because that's not what friends do. I guess.

"I imagine it would be tough. It's tough enough doing this job. I can't imagine having to wear *that*." She nods at what's under my coat. I nod with her.

"It's no picnic. But it pays the bills." Barely. "You married? Got kids?"

"Oh, no. I'm saving up for Europe. I'm going to Italy, might find a rich Italian man to run away with. Who knows?" She laughs, and I try not to choke on my broccoli cheddar. I ponder on how nice it must be to be that delusional, but then I bite my lip hard to punish myself. "How about you?" she asks.

"Married? Was. He died." Her eyes widen. They're gold and green and the whites are streaked with bolts of red lightning. They're the prettiest thing about her.

"Oh my goodness, I'm so sorry...Nancy?"

"Natalie."

"Natalie. That must be really hard." I consider that, if it's any harder now than it was back then. Ol' Nancy doesn't think so.

"Everything's hard. Everything works its way out in the end." *Unless you're your own worst enemy.* I hear it loud and clear, but I know I didn't say it. I look at Tiffan-*ie* who's still wide-eying me. I choke down my last bite of soup and pretend I'm not a crazy person.

"Man, I'm sorry. You guys have any kids?"

"Yes, a daughter. Wren."

"Oh man, what a beautiful name. I've always liked the name 'Claire.' Maybe I can convince my Italian man to go for it!" Her face breaks into a smile, and I almost ask her if she'll take me to her delusional little island where she lives. But then I remember I'm the one hearing voices. "Geez, I better get going. Not sure when Dave will pop back in. That guy's the worst." She rolls her eyes to prove it. "But let's do this again. Maybe the next time you stop by, we can hang out when I get off work."

"I'd love that," I say, knowing I wouldn't, and that I'll never step foot in this place again.

"Take care, Nan...talie." She gives me a wink and hops out of the booth. I pay in cash this time and leave her a barely acceptable tip.

It's not a far walk from the restaurant. It sits at the corner, and there's somebody already light-footing it out of its double-doored mouth. It tickles me, the way people seem like they're floating whenever they walk out of a liquor store. But all I feel is the hard rock of truth in my belly as I find my way in.

Chapter Forty-Three
Rochelle

"She's here," I say. I wait, and I have to wait a beat more than I expect before I hear breathing on the other end.

"Ro, that's amazing." Ann's voice sounds like home. Which is strange because home has shifted. It's this tiny rental house with the carpet that pulls up at the corners and the broken pump outside. Jerry said it would take a week or so before the new one comes in. I walk across the dirty linoleum in the kitchen–dirty no matter how many times I clean it–and I have this strange warmth in my chest because Wren is a mere few streets away.

"Yeah. Yeah it is." But then I think of Natalie. She's like a knot I've been trying to break free with raw fingertips. Every time I touch it, it hurts. Natalie pregnant. Another man. Jerry, with his oiled hair and pleasant face.

Wren.

What has she done?

"When are you going to see them?" I imagine Ann wearing her ridiculous gardening sweater and straw hat even though it's too cold for it now. I've never seen a woman manage to stay so pristine in the sun and dirt.

"I was thinking Sunday. I need time to...process."

"I can imagine." She goes quiet again, an un-Ann-like thing to do. "I saw them."

"Who?"

"Glenn. And that woman." I laugh at her.

"Ann, she's not a dirty word."

"Says you." I roll my eyes to the yellowing ceiling. I should feel gypped, like someone's ripped my life from beneath my feet and has started wearing it for warmth. But I don't. It was the wrong-sized shoe, my old life.

"It's okay, Ann. I forgive them. I really do. They know not what they do and all that jazz. Seriously, I don't even think it fazes them. Which I'm sure is horrifying on its own level. But pearls to swine and all that."

"I've never been a fan of pork," Ann says, the sweater now draped around her shoulders, her hat leaning heavily over one eye.

"Me neither."

Chapter Forty-Four
Wren

I wake up too early on Saturday. The entire week has been absolutely glue-less because as much as I want to ask Rhonda to loan me a twenty, the mere fact that I know her real name feels like we're on a whole other level. I also keep asking myself what Mrs. Ling would think. WWLT.

So I sober my way through the week with only a slight stabbing behind my right eye. It's a little easier knowing I don't have to watch my back for Leslie. She finally makes up with The Preps, but I can tell her face isn't in it. Besides a few lunches together, I don't see her other than the times she flashes by me in the hall. We head nod, but that's about it. I hope she shows up this weekend at Morningside.

Mareck isn't in school. The Redhead is a lone fly buzzing on Leslie's outskirts. I follow her, praying to the Jesus I used to believe in that we meet again somehow. And then we do. In the basement bathroom.

I might as well make it my personal office.

She's shoved herself into a little ball on the floor. It's Friday. Even I believe she should be over him by now.

"Hey," I say, and I get this weird premonition that she'll say "hay is for horses," but she hardly acknowledges my presence. I could really use some glue.

"You know, he was my boyfriend first, and you don't see me still moping about it," I say. She looks up a little. It's the truth. This week's been killer. I've realized when I'm sober, I have to deal with things. So I've done so the best way I know how. Eating a remarkable amount of Slim Jims Jerry keeps stashed in the cabinets and burning photos of Marek in the bathroom sink. The worst part is that Dad doesn't show up anymore.

"Then you never really loved him," she says.

"I find it kind of amusing you fell in love with someone in a matter of hours." She turns at me, and I bite my tongue to keep the realization at bay that even though she's covered in tears and a little bit of snot, she's still ten times prettier than me.

"It wasn't hours," she says. The words are filled with poison, each one shot right into my bloodstream. Oh. So this has been going on for a while now. Perfect.

"Where is he?" I ask. I slide my back down the wall, and she balls up tighter away from me. Her skin is pure white, and I have the same reaction, the knee-jerk need to move away but only because I'm sitting too close to perfection. But I get a glimpse of one of her wrists. The sweater is hiked up and there are faded white slices against the veins there. It's like seeing the Wizard behind the curtain or getting the opportunity to smash your bully right in the face.

I should know.

"Little Rock. Initiation." I wait for this pill of truth to make me gag, but it doesn't. I'm heartbroken on a far different level than I expect. I don't hurt for me. I hurt for Mareck.

And I don't even care that I most definitely won't be seeing my bike again.

The Redhead sniffs, and I want her to wallow in her pain. To suffocate in it. How dare she fall in love with what was mine, the only thing that's kept me alive this whole time. But then I think about the glue and how it's gone. And Dad, how he's gone. And now Mareck. And how no matter all of that, I'm still looking forward to seeing Mrs. Ling. But still, how dare she. And I go to tell her that, but then I see her wrist again.

So instead, my arm finds a way around her shoulders, and I don't even care that she wets my hair with tears.

Chapter Forty-Five
Natalie

The first time I drank I was sixteen and Rebecca was eleven. Our father had leftover peppermint schnapps in the little cabinet above the fridge. He was never a big drinker but his sister in Chihuahua sent it every year because it was "festive." "Tequila's festive, too," he'd say and shake his head as he'd banish it to the back of the cabinet. He was out one Saturday working, and that cabinet started flapping its doors at me. I drank some. A lot of some and let Rebecca have some, too. I wasn't like that. Not back then. But maybe that's wrong. Maybe the demon was there along, and I've just lived this life with the habit of feeding it.

Mack was my next drug. When I could no longer take care of Rebecca, I took care of him, and he drank enough for the both of us. I liked something about that, if I'm being honest. This whole idea of someone actively destroying their life and me being the one to sweep up the pieces. The hero. The one who can be counted on. Lord knows, my mother could never live up to that role.

I swallow a gullet full of vodka to punish myself for that last thought. I'm not even out of the parking lot of the liquor store yet, and the neck of the handle I bought is empty now. The woman couldn't help dying. Lucky her.

The second time I drank was my third week at JCC when the stress of playing manager started to get the best of me. I wasn't well-versed in it yet, so I bought a heavy cabernet that gave me a dull headache and tasted a little like battery acid (not that I've ever tried it). I kept up that charade for a little while. I'd buy a big bottle when grocery shopping, bury it under what little we could afford and avoid Wren's questioning looks. I felt guilt. Duh. I barely had enough money to buy the kid vegetables, but there I was acting like a Beverly Hills housewife in need of an afternoon pick-me-up. I'd drink late at night when Wren was in bed and pretend Mack was sitting next to me.

I don't know if I blame myself anymore. I'm too tired. He was a grown man. He left me, but more importantly, he left his daughter. I play pretend a lot now in other ways. I pretend to be Rochelle. What she must think, how she behaves when someone asks if she has any children. Rochelle in her McMansion living it up with Mr. Augustus. But then I take another swig when I remember she doesn't think at all anymore.

Which is exactly what I try to do, pounding down more of the vodka. I can tell there's a lady sitting in her car next to me. And even though she's sitting in a liquor store parking lot in broad daylight just like me, I can tell she's gone all high and mighty. Like she's better than me because she won't be cracking open those cans until nobody's there to see it. I could do this in the dark, too. But I'm also tired of hiding.

I know this is bad for the baby. No. Fetus. I can't think in terms like that. Because when I do, I see Wren so small and my husband with his inked up hand holding mine. I think about how easily something like family chips and breaks apart. How everything is a beautiful lie. I look over at the lady and wave at her. Throw her a huge smile. She frowns and backs up her car.

Eventually, it's just me alone in the parking lot. I'm used to it but also hate the feeling. I can't even raise the one I got, how am I going to raise a new one? And Jerry isn't even the father. How's that going to feel when we're out and someone congratulates the proud papa? No, this can't happen. I have to fix it. There's a pay phone next to the double doors of the liquor store. It has a phone book chained to it. I could find a clinic, make a call. Do they even accept walk-ins? Worth a shot. But when I go to move my legs, I can't. There's too much comfort in my car, in the act of being alone smack dab in the middle of the world. And if I'm really honest, there's a comfort in the flutter of my belly even if it's too soon for it to roar on its own.

I close my eyes, head against glass and send out a silent plea for someone to come and find me.

Chapter Forty-Six
Rochelle

Dr. Spencer isn't anything like Dr. Cohen. She is small and blonde, and I get the feeling if I look at her the wrong way, she'll break in two. It's not just her thin fame; it's the fact that she's holding herself together with intense concentration, the deep gulley between her eyebrows giving her secret away.

There are no photos on her desk. This is, after all, nothing but business.

"I've looked through everything Dr. Cohen sent. And I've confirmed his findings. It's metastasized to your lungs. I'm afraid we're running out of options." I think about rubbing my finger down the gulley or giving her a hug to hopefully feel her relax. She seems more on edge than I do. And I'm the one dying.

"Fair enough," I say, which I'm sure is odd for her to hear. But why shouldn't it be? I've lived a long life. I've made mistakes. I've found Jesus. I've lost Him on the days I've pondered ending it all, and I found Him again, followed Him to a place called White Smoke where my closest friends are a wound-tight cancer specialist and an A/C repairman. It's all relative and all that jazz.

I feel a little light for some reason. I think maybe because I was worried she'd say I had a ton of options, and then I'd have to sink my teeth into several, weighing the cost of saving my own life. But I'm starting to think that's not how this works nor is that the way this will all go down.

We finish up when there's nothing more to say. She gives me six months. I thank her and smile inside because only God knows the truth behind that.

I'm un-tethered like a balloon when I get into the Jaguar. I grab the car phone and call, not expecting anyone to pick up but then a high, trill voice answers and plucks at my ear drum.

"Augustus residence, where you have to wear that last name to get any respect around here. Can. I. Help. You?" Oh my.

"Um, yes, may I speak to Glenn please?"

"And who, pray tell, may I ask is speaking?" I don't take the bait for fear of her slamming the phone down in my ear.

"Yes, it's his homeowner's insurance agent. I'm just calling to clarify a few things in our new policy."

"Oh. Alright. One sec," Kimber says, and I can hear rooms and wind rush by as she takes the cordless and hunts down Glenn.

"Somebody important," she says, staccato-like, and I imagine she's jabbed the long metal antennae into his side.

"Hello?" He sounds tired. I scold myself when I feel vindicated about it.

"Oh, hi there," I say. The lightness has staked its claim on my voice. "Rochelle?"

"The one and only. Trouble in paradise?" It slips out. I promise.

"Heh...well, you know how the younger ones can get."

"I'm not sure I have much experience in that category, but I'm sure you know how to handle yourself."

"Yeah, well, I had thought so..." Glenn's an old man, and for the first time, I can finally hear it.

"Well, I won't be long. I just wanted to give you an update. One, I've found Natalie."

"Really? What's she like after all these years?"

"Well, I haven't seen her in person, but she's knocked up with some guy's baby and not the guy she's living with. So I'd say...changed."

"I'd have to agree with you on that one. Wren still with her, I imagine?"

"Yeah, she is. I'm working up the courage, Glenn. It's been a long time."

"It has," he says, almost sad.

"Oh and one more thing. I'm dying. Officially, I guess."

"As are the rest of us. You're just getting a bit of a head start." I laugh until I'm the one

who's sad now. "I miss you, Rochelle," he says.

"I miss you, too, Glenn." In the background Kimber is throwing verbal darts.

"Your next check is coming soon. If you need anything–"

"I know, Glenn."

"Okay. I love you, and, well, you really don't know how sorry I am." Something sounds like it's been flung against the wall.

"I'm starting to realize that," I say and hang up on the man who used to mean everything.

Chapter Forty-Seven
Wren

Rhonda came bright and early, way before we were to hit Morningside. She lightly pawed the front door like a small mouse, which wasn't necessary. Mom and Jerry were already at work, and I was in the living room watching *Recess* and eating half a poptart. I invited her in and offered her the other half while we watched cartoons in silence. And then it wasn't so silent.

"My mom's getting an abortion." It's something I don't need to be talking to Rhonda about, but I can't tell Jerry, and my mother's zipped in and out like a fairy on acid this week. She's not all there, and it makes me miss her.

There's a million answers swimming the shoreline of Rhonda's face but all she says is, "Oh, okay."

"She's not a bad person."

"You don't have to convince me."

"I was trying to convince myself."

"Not to outdo you or anything, but my mom died when I was ten. Cancer. And before that she was a partier. Alcohol, coke even. Here. White Smoke. Of all places. And the principal's wife." She talks to the leftover quarter of pop tart in her hand. "My mom."

Coke. I start to remember who Rhonda's mother is. She helped get my mom arrested although Mom wasn't doing much to save herself from the situation. I remember playdates, trips to the mall. I remember Rhonda's curly hair.

I remember Rhonda. But I like her too much to have to tell her the truth.

So instead, I ask, "What was she like?" even though I know on some level. Loud. I remember her being loud. But on so many others, I don't. Because it's always like that with people. You can know a million different shades of someone while somebody else has been wading in their gray for far too long.

"I made her be the moments she loved me. All the rest I clipped away and let my Dad handle." She puts her poptart in her mouth and chews thoughtfully with her mouth closed. That would be nice, I think. To have a dad handle it.

It was a quiet ride to Morningside. I looked out for Leslie, but she never showed. Instead, I stood next to Aleski Bjorkland who kept pointing at the curtains and saying "sheets." Finally, a nurse came and shepherded us to the dining room where the residents were gathered for a 50's sock hop. I do the math and realize a lot of the residents were roughly in their thirties during the 50's. I try not to roll my eyes.

"There she is," Mrs. Ling says behind me. I turn, and she's sitting in a pink sweater and pearls at a table with two other ladies. "They tried to put one of those, what do you call them? Poodle skirts on me. I told them it would be the death of them." She smiles and reveals her small, white teeth. I smile back and sit next to her. And I weigh the feeling in my chest. Relief.

We watch the parade of nonsense before us for a little while. The nurses and events director are dressed up in what I'm assuming is their best sock hop garb, dancing and twirling around. It makes me a little sad. Like this is all I'll have to look forward to one day.

"Oh it's not all bad," Mrs. Ling says, reading my thoughts. "We get Jell-O on Saturdays," she says and lifts her taupe plastic bowl of green slime. She laughs, and I do, too. She looks peaceful.

"How can you be happy?" It comes out all philosophical, like I'm trying to expose the root of an issue plaguing all of mankind.

"Well, I'm the only one in charge of something like that. And I'm not always a fan of the alternative."

"But how can you be happy when everything sucks? When everything's beyond your control?"

Mrs. Ling nods. She considers the question with a soft face, but she gives a hard look. "Your circumstances aren't where joy is, Wren. Joy is only found in Jesus." One of the ladies at the table nods, overhearing Mrs. Ling. There's a wet trail snaking down to her chin.

"What does that even mean?" There's something inside of me that rolls its eyes at that statement. Something that doesn't even feel like it's a part of me. But I defer to it, the way it elbows out all my other thoughts and sits fat in my brain. Why would I ever give up control to someone else? To a man no less? I think we already know where trusting the opposite sex has gotten me.

"It means giving everything, your thoughts, your heart, your life, your decisions, giving all of them to God. As much as you think you can outwit a situation, you can't. It's there. It's looking at you like a cat looks at a dish of milk. It will lap you up. But God is the cat's owner. You put your faith in Him, and He locks up the cat. Or He leaves the cat so you get the opportunity to silence your fear. Either way, it's His game. And we all play our part. Some very well with His help. Others, slowly sinking.

I have a hard time looking into her eyes, but when I do, I'm swallowed by another wave of relief. I wore my good pants today, the only pair I have that doesn't have holes or safety pins running through them. For once, I'm dressed like I can actually process the world around me. And something Mrs. Ling says takes hold.

"I used to believe in Jesus."

"You never stopped," says Mrs. Ling. "You just hid Him so you don't have to look Him in the face."

We watch the makeshift sock hop end, and I'm suddenly overwhelmed by the smell of fifty bowls of Jell-O. We spend more time as a group playing bingo after the plates are cleared. We chat for a bit. The woman who was crying is named Bonnie. Her husband Dwayne died last month, and she says the only thing that gets her through is her faith. She pats her Jell-O -stained napkin at her eyes, her mouth.

Something in me elbows hard, and there's a radiating pain at the front of my forehead.

It's time to leave. I hug Mrs. Ling and tell her goodbye. I say thank you, which I think is barely audible, but she fires back with a strong, "Don't thank me. I'm only the messenger."

In the car, Rhonda fires up the engine and gives me the once over. "You look different."

"It's because I am," I say.

Chapter Forty-Eight
Natalie

I thought it was magic, Jerry scooping me into his van. He appeared in bits and pieces, flashes of frown and determination as he worked me out of my car and into his passenger side seat. The liquor store owner apparently asked me who he could call to pick me up, and I was somehow coherent enough to tell him. The fact that he didn't call the cops is a small miracle. Jerry told me he went back later with a work buddy, told him my car wouldn't start, and when they got to the liquor store, the thing magically turned over. The work buddy thinks I was buying wine for a béarnaise.

Oh Jerry.

The truth is that I was buying alcohol to kill myself. At least the little pieces that still hold onto everything I've lost. But you can't tell a person that. You can't tell them you're made of more than flesh and blood, but also the secrets and sadness that make you stumble-drunk in a liquor store parking lot.

Even I think I'm evil.

Wren wasn't home. Thank the gods, the heavens, the big floating nothingness above our heads. She thinks she hates me now, just wait until she catches a whiff of what I've done. I know what it's like to live with an alcoholic, wishing things will change. And for her, they finally did. But I'm not even sure for the better.

Smelling myself in this bed, I have to go with the alternative.

Jerry's out there somewhere on the couch. Wren came home. I could hear her and Jerry talking in the living room, but she didn't come looking for me. He must have told her I was sick, which is true on many levels. It's still inside me, the fetus. The clump of cells. I keep forcing the image of a black tumorous cyst choking off my organs but the image won't hold. Instead, I see the tiny fuzzy shape of a small human being like they showed me on Wren's ultrasound. My tears mix with sweat because even though I know it's drafty in my room, vodka always makes me a billion times hotter. It feels like I've tripped and landed in a deep hole and there's barely any room to breathe. It feels like I'm looking up and can only see a small orb of light pounding down onto my forehead.

I roll around for a while, wading through a sea of sheets. I argue with myself or the gods or the heavens or the great big nothingness that I know hovers dark and heavy above our apartment complex. "What do you want from me?" I whisper because I know it's there, and it always has been.

I just don't know what it is.

Chapter Forty-Nine
Rochelle

I realize I'm dressed like I'm going to a funeral. I'm wearing my black pants and gray sweater and pearls at my ears. I swim a little bit in my clothes, the weight loss hitting harder this time than the last. I look in the mirror and don't see Rochelle but someone who would prompt others to go "Is that Rochelle? She kind of looks like her but...not really." I'm starting to forget what I actually look like.

But I'm starting to remember it doesn't even matter.

I feel Him at my shoulder. Jesus. Glenn's not here, so I can talk freely, and boy, do I give Him an earful. He knows how scared I am. How sorry. How worried I am that this is all going to blow up in my face. I imagine a non-believer sneaking up on me to watch the ravings of a lunatic. And maybe they're right on some level. But definitely not for trusting Christ.

I'm all ready, and there's a sense of comfort where bone feeds into bone in the middle of my chest. I know it's going to be okay before it even plays out before my eyes. So I rest in that. I find my Bible. I used to do this thing where I'd run my finger through it to receive some sort of inspiration when I needed it, but it would undoubtedly always land in Leviticus. So instead, I go to an old favorite.

The Lord is near to the brokenhearted and saves the crushed in spirit. There. I say and pray a million prayers under my breath.

I wish I could call Jerry and let him know I'm on my way, but I wasn't smart enough to grab his number. He knows I'm coming or at least assumes it. I hope.

I pull up to the apartment complex. It sits in Sunday morning sunlight, but that does it no favors. The buildings are painted in pastel colors as if each one is a past-due Easter egg. The paint peels. The sidewalks crack into tiny bits of rock. There's a man in a black hoodie smoking a cigarette, watching me roam around the parking spaces with his hidden eyes. This is home for my Wren.

I want to blame Glenn. I want to think that I was sucked into his vortex having to care for him and be the trophy when I should have been checking up on my granddaughter no matter what it took. But Glenn is powerless. I know that. I'm the one with the choice. And I'm the one who chose poorly.

Again, there's comfort there. Past is past. This is now.

I find the right building and make my way up, ignoring the gentleman in the hoodie who sits stout like a chimney. I'm wearing my black felt coat and clutch my hand bag like an old lady. But then I remember I'm not far from that label. But no matter. I stand straighter and push ahead when I remember the girl near the tree, looking up.

A wave of smells hits me. Food cooking, grease. Languages I don't understand. When I find it, number thirteen, I give myself a few moments to realize what it is I'm about to do.

My fist works without listening to my heart, and I find it knocking on the door without my permission. I hold my breath. And then Jerry answers the door.

"Rochelle," he says. He looks distressed, his memory snapping into place. "That's right, you were coming by today."

"Is it a bad time?" *Please say it isn't*, I think. I don't think I can do this again. He pauses, thinks about it. But Jerry and I both know he's not one to turn someone away.

"No, no come in. Just give me one second." He ushers me inside into a cramped foyer with bars on one side and an accordion door on the other. He moves off to the right, down a hall. When I look straight and over to the left, I see her. Wren.

"Mimi?" she asks. She's herself but not. It looks like someone's vandalized her with makeup and a poor wardrobe. She's wearing spaghetti straps, and even though we're inside, I can feel the draft in this place even under my coat. Her eyes are ringed round with eyeliner and her lips are stained. Faded. She looks...used.

"Little duck." I move to the kitchen table where she sits with an oversized Tupperware bowl and plastic spoon. She's fishing out off brand Lucky Charms and has made a pile of marshmallows next to the bowl. I can't feel my heart.

"What are you doing here?" I've practiced this, rehearsed it so many times, I think the answer will be robotic. But it gets stuck in my throat. There's a stud in her nose and rings in the cartilage of her ear. It looks like...punishment.

"I...well, I–"

"Rochelle." If I wasn't ready for Wren, I'm definitely not prepared for Natalie. She's dressed in an open bathrobe, shorts, and a thrown-on tee underneath. She literally looks like Jerry went and pried her off the road.

"Oh, I'm sorry. I didn't know you were sick."

"I'm fine," she says, bringing a delicate hand to her temple. "Rough night."

"Oh, sure," I say, wondering what that means in her world. I pray her sobriety is still in check.

"Why don't we sit in the living room," she says. I follow her, wanting to hug her and Wren and rescue them from this place although I'm not sure what I'd be rescuing them from. Jerry seems harmless. But it's obvious hurt's holding them captive and writing its will all over their faces. Natalie won't stop wincing.

"I...I know it's strange I'm here. I've missed you both." I look at Wren who looks down at her bowl. She's sixteen now, but I can't find that on her other than her outward shell. The inside seeps out, in her downturned eyes and her hands that she's brought back to her and rests in her lap. She looks like she hasn't been hugged in a very long time.

"That's an understatement," Natalie says bluntly. This is the Natalie I remember from last time when Wren and I would visit her after the arrest. She'd sit on one of the white couches in the recovery clinic and icily hunt me down with her eyes. She's changed, different than when she was with Mack. And I know I'm a terrible person if I blame her. But I was just hoping nine years had worked some sort of magic. Suddenly, I feel it again. My heart.

"I'm not doing too well," I start. I can see Wren shift in my periphery. "The cancer's back. It's incurable this time." It's too quiet but Jerry pierces it by rustling his way into one of the back rooms. "And I left Glenn." I process this information the same time Natalie does. It's never real until you can say it out loud.

"Well, if you're looking for a place to stay, we're a little cramped at Chez Reynolds." Natalie lifts her hand like Vanna White. "We obviously have yet to win the lottery."

"I'm not looking for a place to stay. Glenn found a place for me. Divorce isn't final yet, but we've worked out a system."

"One where he pays you off?" *She's hurt*, I have to remind myself. I keep my bitterness at bay, the way I feel that she just kicked me to the curb once she was set free. I wanted to help her get on her feet. We offered to set her up for success. But she quickly knocked down anything I suggested.

"I came here to reconnect with you, with Wren. I just...I'm so sorry, Natalie. I'm sorry I haven't kept in touch, but I also know you didn't want that."

"No, no don't even Rochelle. Don't play the victim. We all know how good you are at that one. But I won't let you unleash that kind of monster, not in my...home." She glances around and puckers her lips like she's tasted a lemon. "If you had wanted to stay, you would have. But you had to go back to Glenn and your pile of money, taking off in that Jaguar of yours like you were riding off into the sunset. Well, I don't consider you much of a hero, Rochelle. Your granddaughter's missed you for a very long time." We both look at Wren, which is a mistake. She gets up from the table and heads back to wherever Jerry headed to.

"Maybe," I say. And I think about it. Maybe she's right. On some level, I wanted to be the hero. I had ruined things with Mack. I had made a mess of him, and maybe I thought this was my redemption. My heart throbs inside of me–spastic like it's going to break free. Maybe I wanted to prove I had something to offer. And maybe I just wanted to go home to Glenn because, at the time, he was the only one I could run to.

Natalie quickly looks up. I can tell she's surprised. She shuts her robe closed with both hands and her eyes look like they're sorting through multiple options. "Rochelle, I don't know what's happened." She curves over a little bit, a tiny "c" in her spine. I almost go to touch her, but I don't want her to stop talking. "This isn't anywhere near where I thought we'd land. And I had tried so hard. I mean really. Even with the whole arrest thing, before that, I mean I know I screwed up. But I had a plan. I had worked hard. I was going to do so much and give Wren so much. But look at me." And I do. She's herself but hardened. She's who she's always been but a rougher, worn out version. I wish I could lift that burden from her, but I'm only human.

"I know, Natalie. You've always been so resilient, such a hard worker. But take it from someone who hasn't exactly landed where she thought she would either. Sometimes, doing it your own way blows up in your face. But only if you're lucky."

"What does that mean?" I think of Glenn. How he's always riding high even if there's some young thing chirping at him like an angry little bird.

"It means there are those of us who skirt through life, building our own destinies. Castles in the sand, really. But God allows it, keeps the structures nice and strong so we can stand at the top and pat our backs, looking at everything we've created." I think of being smack dab in the middle of my marriage to Glenn. How good it felt to live in the big house. To host all those parties. To sit at the pool and see my reflection and smile. "But then there are the rest of us. The ones who try to build what God knocks down, repeatedly sometimes. And it's easy to get angry. To look over the fence and wonder why your neighbor still has it so good while you're left on your rump to comb through the broken pieces of everything you tried to make. But that's the kicker. It was all trial and error. And God knows the only way He'll bring us to Him is if we're left to sift through our mistakes."

"Broken," Natalie says. She takes her hands to her stomach.

"'Even our brokenness is for God's good. God can take the bad things in life and use them for His purposes,'" I say, quoting Romans.

"That's good. You should put that in a book."

"Fortunately, one's already been written," I say. I smile at her. I chance it, moving my hand behind her shoulder blades. She looks at me.

"Rochelle. How long?" Her question could refer to anything, but I know she's asking how much longer I have on this earth.

"Only as long as He'll allow."

Chapter Fifty
Wren

Mimi.

It's like being hit with a wave and trying not to drown. She's dying. That's the worst part. Obviously. No, the worst part is that up until now, she hasn't been dying, and I haven't been able to see her.

The hate is loose and looking for a target. And all I see is Mom.

But I grab my dirty sweatshirt and walk-run right past Natalie Reynolds moping on the couch. Sorry your life is a sinking ship, lady, but I'm tired of hanging off the side.

I don't mean that.

I find Mimi almost at her car. The Jaguar. After all these years. She walks too slow like every step hurts. I walk behind her slowly, too. I don't want to scare her.

"Mimi," I whisper and then clear my throat. "Mimi." I say it louder, definitively the second time, and she turns around. I try to ignore the creeper sitting fat on his haunches in his hoodie, watching us like a movie.

"Wren." She walks towards me, and I meet her halfway. She smells as she always does as I hug her, but she feels different. Too skinny.

"I'm sorry," I say.

"For what?"

"For anything she said in there." A small bubble escapes her. A laugh.

"Oh, she didn't say anything I can't handle. Your mom's...had it rough."

"I guess that just means she needs to hop in line." I stare down the hoodie who's pinching a cigarette. He's a black smoke stack against our powder blue building.

"I'll try not to elbow anyone in the process." She looks at me, and it's like seeing the past. A ghost. I miss Dad.

"She's pregnant, you know." And then my eyes become traitors, and I'm crying. I guess I'm growing up and that maturity thing is smacking me hard with its fat hand because I'm not the saddest about myself. I'm the saddest about the baby my mother's stupidly growing, and I'm not sure what I'm more worried about: if it dies or if it lives.

"I know," Mimi says and takes me in her arms again. I'm lost there. I don't know how I'm going to add this all up in my head and be okay with it. There's nobody left. Literally. Except for Mimi, and I know she'll be gone soon, too. It's what everyone does.

"I'm going to miss you." The words clink out of my mouth like falling change.

"You have no idea," she says. She pulls me off, and I feel like an octopus clinging. She finds my eyes and says, "Remember when you were little, and I was taking you to church. And I said, 'Don't look at me, look at Jesus?'"

"Yeah," I say, faintly remembering. I remember the dresses she bought me from Dillard's and the way she curled my hair. I felt like a princess and would sit with her. I had a hard time understanding what the pastor was saying, but afterwards, she took me for pancakes and milkshakes, and she would break it down. And it kind of always felt like she was saying that nothing had to be a burden, if I didn't want it to be.

"Hold on to that. Hold on to the hope in that, Wren. Because there will come a time when someone will fill every little part of you, and you'll confuse yourself. You'll start to think that who they are and their actions define what it is you were made to be. But only Christ can do that. You have to hold onto that. You have to believe with your whole being that only He covers all wounds. Otherwise you break off. You shrivel up. And there will be nothing left to give."

"Okay," I say, but I feel six again, trying to define every word she's thrown at me.

"He loves you, Wren. It starts there, with fully knowing that."

"But If He loves me He wouldn't have done this to me." I stare at the smokestack again, but he shrugs off the B movie we're making. He grunts his way up the stairs.

"No? Love isn't necessarily getting what you want. Sometimes, love is an absence of it. Trust me. I'm the queen of receiving and watching it all be taken away. And guess which one saved my life?"

Her eyes almost scare me. She's looking into me, and it's foreign. If you have to lose everything to save your life, I should have nine of them right about now.

"Mimi?"

"I love you," she says. And for a second, I almost understand.

Chapter Fifty-One
Natalie

It felt like being on an episode of *This is Your Life*, and when I looked around, I wasn't impressed.

Can't imagine what an audience would think.

Rochelle. After all these years. I saw Mack in an instant. Felt him, too. And I wanted to die. How dare she dredge up that kind of memory? How dare she open that door after all this time? And yeah, I know, it's not like I had locked him up. He's always been inside my head, roaming about. But to see her was too close to seeing his face. His questioning eyes. I just wouldn't want him to blame himself. Even though sometimes, that's the only person I blame.

Then she sat next to me to tell me she's dying, when frankly, I had already grieved her. Okay, so you saunter in here, get your granddaughter's hopes up and then tell us you're about to kick the bucket. I could taste the anger in my teeth. What do I do with that, Rochelle? What can I possibly do? I almost asked her to leave when Wren got up and headed to her room, but I kept my cool. Stood my ground. We were going to finish this.

But then she talked about being broken. And my entire body lit on fire. I don't know how to explain it. It started at the crown of my head and lit up my cells and organs like a slowly moving pour of lava. All my insides started to scream, and I was afraid she was going to hear it. That part. That part about looking over the fence? Mary. It reminded me of my dead ex-friend. Sheesh, how many people can say that? But I remember looking over her fence one too many times and wondering how someone can have so much but appreciate so little.

And then it made me think of me.

Things. I don't have a lot of those. I know the way women look at me. I know because I look at myself the same way. But then I look at

Wren, and I sometimes think, *How can I be so lucky?* Which makes no sense in the world. I'm thirty-seven and working at a glorified Hooters for crying out loud. But I am. I know that. Even here on my knees in the absolute thick of it.

Even as my fingers touch all these broken bits of me.

I *am* lucky. And I want to thank someone for that. But I've always had a hard time pinning down exactly who.

God. Rochelle talks so freely about Him. Her? I don't even know. But hearing that name come out of her mouth, the fire consumed me. I felt known. Like, even here on this couch, Rochelle gone, and Wren still in her room, I feel incinerated and yet? Still whole.

But different. New.

If she's turned me into a Christian, I'll spit.

Epilogue

S he fought. She wasn't counting on that. But there was something about living in a cheap rental and her granddaughter wearing too much eyeliner that forced Rochelle to snatch at little bits of life while the cancer broke her down. She went to church, a small non-denominational one in Junction that didn't seem to take a hard stance against lipstick. She invited Wren. And Wren went because she couldn't stand staying in the apartment with a woman she couldn't talk to. Her mother was still a mess but this time, a mess that kept to herself in her room. Jerry went out a lot to who knows where. And Wren? She was angry enough at me to talk.

"I hate you," she said one day after stealing a ten from Jerry's wallet. She bought glue, and we walked to the edge of the park and sat at the skinny fishing dock that stretches into the lake. There were ducks there and green water that crystallized in the sun.

"I know," I say. She sniffs it and nonchalantly like she was wiping her nose. There were joggers and women with strollers and children screaming everywhere. But we were sitting tight inside a bubble, Wren and me.

"You did all of this."

"I can't say that's accurate."

"You didn't stop it."

"Now that part's accurate." She'd been thinking on me in her heart. It's the type of thought that always comes when you're at the end of yourself and everyone else for that matter. It's the type of thought my beautiful Mack had right at the last moment.

"So what do I do?"

"See, that question doesn't even resonate, does it? *You* can't do anything."

"Way to crack that case, Sherlock." She winces. "Sorry."

"No offense taken. What I'm saying is that I'm the one that fixes this, Wren. The only one. And until you can come to terms with that, well, you'll still be clawing your way up the sides of the pit. And those are some very tall walls, my friend." She sniffs again, a long one this time. Nods.

"You're going to have to stop that, you know. It clouds your brain, tears it apart. And you're going to need a strong mind for the next phase of all of this. Not to mention, a strong heart."

"Yeah, I figured. Nothing's easy."

"Would you want it to be?" Wren laughs and a tear takes its time down her face.

"I want to say 'yes' to that question. But something tells me the answer's 'no.'"

"Ding, ding, ding," I whisper and hold her close as another tear catches up with its friend.

• • • •

ROCHELLE IS MOVED TO hospice. Wren calls her grandfather who sounds different, not so sure of himself. She can hear something shrill in the background that sounds like the cross between a banshee and someone who's lost their meds. But her grandfather tells her he has everything covered financially in that matter of fact way of his and says, "I hope you're doing well, Wren." There's nothing she can coherently say to this, so she fumbles her way off the phone.

Poor Mimi, she thinks.

But Mimi doesn't think the same. She's in bed staring at the ceiling. She just got off the phone with Ann who cried enough rivers for the both of them to sail down. She'll miss her friend. That's true. But she looks forward to seeing her again and wonders if obnoxiously large hats are allowed on the new earth. I think I can make an exception.

The final moments are hard ones but not for Rochelle. Natalie refuses to come. Wren hates her for it, but it's not because Natalie is cold-hearted. She just can't do it. She just can't watch Rochelle lose consciousness. She can't do another funeral. But ultimately, she will do another funeral because guilt eats at her bones, and she can't leave Wren alone with all that pain. Rhonda drives Wren and sits helplessly in a chair while Wren holds Mimi's hand. Wren watches her past and her rock float away, and she's devastated but not hopeless. Mimi helped her understand the new earth and being with the Lord until Christ returns and how we'll all be together again if Wren wants it that way. She's decided she does.

They look like two lumps of coal, Natalie and Wren, sitting on the pew at Rochelle's funeral. It's a small affair that surprisingly Glenn Augustus shows up for. He hangs in the back with Jerry who doesn't know what to do with his hands. Rochelle didn't want to go back to Texas. She wanted to stay here and be cremated and buried wherever Wren thought fit. She explained this to Ann who cried so hard she was expecting to vomit, but Rochelle said, "This is the right choice. And I know you know that. I also know you know this is a small blip in the big picture. Keep your eyes on the big picture, Ann." And Ann promised she would.

I walk with them, Natalie and Wren, as they go up and look at Rochelle. They say goodbye in a funeral home that is empty save for themselves and Jerry and Glenn Augustus who is watching his entire life crash over his head but is too stubborn to do anything about it. He leaves softly while they peer into Rochelle's quiet face.

After it's done, the cremation, Wren is given the urn which is really a box. It has Rochelle's date of living and her full name: Rochelle Diana Reynolds. No "Augustus" even though the divorce was never finalized. She wanted to go back to the beginning, which is something you really can't do. But you can look forward to the light that will most likely set you on fire.

And take that first step.

Wren holds onto it in her room. Natalie doesn't say anything. Wren looks at it, and figures it's time to take that step. She calls Rhonda and Rhonda calls Mrs. Ling. Mrs. Ling, who has always been a very persuasive woman in her own way, talks to the activities director at Morningside who runs wild with the idea. Philip isn't a believer, but a man intent on drama. He was never accepted into NYU to major in stage theater, so he makes Morningside his stage. He calls the preacher who administers communion to the residents on Sundays and finds a metal wash tub he sets in the middle of the dining hall. He works his "magic," and when he's done, the place looks absolutely ridiculous. But the thing is, it doesn't even matter. Wren's already plucked the heart from her chest and put it in my hands. It doesn't matter how much white taffeta Phillip uses to "juze up" the windows. It doesn't matter that the wash tub is a tad too small so Wren will be shoving herself down into it like a coiled snail shell. What matters is that she trusts me.

And when I knocked, she opened.

She's wet and her muscles train to hold tight into a painful ring. The pastor "dunks" her, half an inch of water grazing over her face and body. And when she comes up and opens her eyes, she's looking past the fluorescent lighting into a whole new world of possibility. And I am right there with her.

Afterwards, she eats cake with Mrs. Ling and Rhonda and they talk about Mimi. She lightly touches on Natalie who she didn't even invite, let alone tell. "Two baptisms? What, the first one didn't take?" She could already hear her mother's frustration coming from the cave of her bedroom. Natalie quit Double Dees and has been living off Jerry's good graces, something she vowed never to do. But she seems broken now, troubled. Wren wonders if she can feel the rocks at the bottom with the tips of her toes.

After she finishes her piece (which came from a large sheet cake in the shape of a very pink cross), she watches Phillip interpret his mistaken understanding of baptism with a dance he choreographed last night. And Wren laughs at how everybody always seems to get everything oh so wrong.

• • • •

NATALIE SWEATS IN HER room. She feels inhuman. It's been happening for a few nights now, and she doesn't know what it is or why it's happening.

The demons.

I've allowed them to come out where she can see them. And they can feel me in the corner watching as they tread the ground, some with pointed hooves, others with thick talons. One even looks like an alien, a pure white being with deep slanted eyes. That one thinks he's the king of deception. They keep watch, not trusting me, yet reveling in their good fortune. I let them revel. They won't be doing it for long.

The first one, Natalie chalks up to a bad night's sleep. But it's there under the surface, her inability to move and the hot breath wrapping around her throat. The next few nights she's come unleashed a little. She stops brushing her teeth, and Jerry sleeps alone on the couch. She wants to yell out to him when it happens, but she can't. I keep her body paralyzed and her voice quiet. She needs to fully know and understand what she's messing with. Evil.

And evil ceases for no one but me.

But eventually, I call them off. She's left a sweaty mess one night, forcing every cell to stay awake so she doesn't have to experience whatever that was again. She starts talking. I listen.

"I-I'm, you know..."

"No. I don't."

"Sorry. I'm so sorry." She's messy in her sweat and knotted hair and bad breath but to me, she looks beautiful in this shade of vulnerable.

"Yes. That I know." She's thinking about everything she's lost with the power of her own hands. She misses her husband and father and the sister who still thinks of her in Texarkana. She looks at the future like it's a deep dark nothing and fear starts to eat her heart again.

But then, I tip her chin up.

• • • •

ONE DAY, NATALIE COMES alive. She leaves her room while Jerry works and Wren silently prays through school. She showers and brushes her hair into a braid down her back. She puts on her "fat pants" the only pair of jeans she owns that doesn't cut off her circulation and a cream turtleneck sweater Rochelle had gotten her one Christmas long ago. She finds her boots, and her coat and gathers things into her purse. And then she finds Rochelle's ashes and puts them in the crook of her arm.

She goes for a drive. She takes what she believes is still Rochelle to TGI Fridays. She stashes her in her bag and gets waited on by a guy named Kevin because Tiffanie doesn't work week days. No matter. Natalie wants things to be different and feels this is a good sign. After Kevin delivers her broccoli cheddar soup and leaves her be, she takes Rochelle out and places her on the other side of the table in her tucked away booth.

"Thank you for agreeing to meet with me." Natalie gives a wicked a grin. "I mean, I know you didn't have much choice, but I needed to talk to you." She quiets as Kevin comes by to refill her water and pretends to not see the box on the table.

"Sorry about that. Waiters," she says, remembering she was one what feels like a lifetime ago. "My father told me a bible verse once. 'The foolishness of man perverteth his way: and his heart fretteth against the Lord.' At the time, I thought he was babbling. We didn't go to church growing up. I've never gone to church as an adult. But when he said it...it was like a sword piercing right through my middle. It worried me. It sat inside me a long time, and there would be moments that phrase would pop out at me, and I'd just shove it way in the back.

Why should I care what the Lord thinks? I don't believe in the Lord. But I still couldn't stop caring and worrying. And it was so frustrating because I couldn't figure out why I felt that way." Natalie stops and swallows another mouthful of soup. She's gotten very hungry and so has the baby inside her. The baby she tries to ignore.

"I know you believe in God, Rochelle. And I'm less inclined now to think you've lost your marbles. I've seen, I've seen the evil at night." Kevin walks by on his way to the kitchen and starts to worry he won't be getting a tip.

"I can see it now. And I'm giving it all up. I can't stop it. I can't do it on my own. I can't." She says again, her face wet with fear. But I place my hand on her back and the string of words hits her where the sword used to stay put. *But I can.*

"I know, I think. I'm starting to realize that. But I don't know where to begin." *Wren.* She nods and swallows the taste of broccoli. "Yeah, okay. You're right. Rochelle, if you see Mack. And please say you see him. Let him know how sorry I am. How I failed him and how I should have been okay with just...being." I hold her, and she nods her head into my shoulder. She can feel me, truly, and she starts to weep with a pure and grateful heart.

Kevin starts to walk toward the table with the check, giving up all hope.

• • • •

IT WAS A LONG DAY OF prayer, so a headache rattles against the edges of her skull. Rhonda had a doctor's appointment so Wren prepares for the long walk back to the apartment. But as she exits, she sees her mother, and she's never looked more beautiful.

"What are you doing here?" she asks. Her mom's showered, and her face is light with makeup. Her hair is braided and she's wearing a top that's always sat crumpled in the back of her closet. Wren's ashamed to think how she looks like a real mom.

"I just had this feeling I needed to see you." They move toward the parking lot, pass The Yard on their way. Wren stares at it a bit too long, remembering the sweet release of everything through one simple punch. But then she sees Leslie waving at her from the parking lot, and she weakly waves back. Maybe simple isn't always best.

"About?" Wren asks.

Natalie's eyes semi-circle around her daughter. "Where's your bike?"

"You first."

"Fine. Facing the aftermath of...everything." They get inside the car, and Natalie fires it up. Warm air blasts at both of them. She starts to drive.

"How do you suppose we do that?"

"I haven't figured it out yet. And I'm not going to. I'm going to leave that up to..." Natalie purses her lips and glances at the rearview mirror. Something flashes brightly at her. "Him."

"O....kay? Who's this "him"? Are you seeing "*him*" right now?"

"Shut up," Natalie laughs and smacks Wren on the arm. Wren smiles. She's missed her mom. "God. I'm leaving it up to God."

Wren's smile freezes. She says it before she can think about it. "I got baptized last week."

"Again? The first one didn't take?" Like clockwork. This time, it's Wren's turn to smack.

"No...I don't know. My heart wasn't in it last time. I think I just did it because I wanted to be like Mimi. But now...I want to be like Jesus." Natalie glances at her daughter, tries to pin down what seems so different about her.

"That's good, Wren. I mean, I don't know how all this is supposed to work, but at least it feels better. At least I'm not covered in chicken grease getting cat-called by a bunch of wannabe hunters."

"There is that," Wren says. She watches the world whip by them through the window. "Mareck," she adds. "Gone forever."

"Sucks about the bike," Natalie says. "But good riddance."

"Something like that."

They pass their apartment complex, and Wren starts to question where they're going. But then she just sits back and enjoys the ride. A little while later they end up at the Wal-Mart in Junction.

"Well, I suppose first thing's first," Natalie says. "Time to get you a new coat."

• • • •

THE NEXT STEPS HAPPEN with little effort on Natalie's part. And she figures that's probably why they feel so right. She calls her sister. She knows if the line is disconnected or Rebecca doesn't answer, then that's one road she won't be traveling. But if she does, well...

"Hello?" Rebecca sounds the same, and for a moment, Natalie is back to the day she learned her father died.

"Hi." She starts to explain who she is, but Rebecca starts crying.

"Well, it took you long enough didn't it? What's wrong? Economy too unstable to sell that mansion of yours?"

"Something like that. Look–"

"Don't you 'look' me. You don't have anything to say to make this better."

"You're right. I absolutely don't, Rebecca. All I can say is I'm so sorry. I shouldn't have ever left. I should have stayed home to be with you and Dad." She remembers her father and the flood gates open. He knew, but he let her make her own decision.

Rebecca goes quiet on the phone. She wants to hold on to her own self-righteousness, but she can feel it slipping away. Antonio is thirteen and giving her a run for her money, and Steven left a few months ago, and she hasn't told anyone. She wants to tell her sister.

"Can you forgive me?"

Rebecca takes in a lungful of breath and sighs out, "Always."

• • • •

"MY SISTER NEEDS ME," is how she puts it to Jerry. Jerry has a clean heart, a good soul. But he's been putting stock in a woman when he knows that time and commitment belong to me. He nods his head, sitting in the kitchen, a plate of untouched jerky sitting between them like an offering. He feels like the sacrifice. Like the one who always gets the raw end of the deal.

"That's fine, Natalie. You go. I figured this would happen eventually anyways," he says, trying his best not to sound bitter.

"Jerry I'm so grateful for you. So is Wren. You've done nothing but treat us with kindness and respect. And I haven't done the same. I've been terrible to you, Jerry. I've wasted your time and money making you think that we're some sort of makeshift family. But I never committed to that like I should have. But I think it's a good thing I didn't. I wasn't honest with myself. I was miserable. And I feel like for the first time I have a chance to be better. To do better. And I have to face my consequences before I know how to be a good wife again. I just feel this pull to go back and face my demons.

Jerry nods again because that he understands. He thinks of his mother for a fleeting moment, the only kind he lets himself think when it comes to her. She hurt him. The woman allowed evil to consume her. And he knows he's been using Natalie like a human security blanket. He has to do the same thing. Face his demons even if he's afraid they'll swallow him whole.

"Jerry, you're better at this whole thing than I am. I know how you feel about God. And I know deep down you're willing to trust Him to put you right where you belong." He looks at her, a question in his eyes. Such a beautiful woman who suddenly starts to speak his same language. The pang of loss is so real inside of him. But so is knowing I always have a way of working things out.

• • • •

TEXARKANA. WREN DOESN'T want to leave Rhonda and Jerry and Mrs. Ling but that's about it. She buried Mareck a long time ago, so setting foot on old soil feels like something she needs. It's something Natalie needs too.

When she packs up her room, Wren finds trash and old socks balled up in a corner of her closet, and underneath, the plastic eyes of an old furry friend. Wren smiles.

They stay with Aunt Rebecca who's grateful for the company. Wren doesn't take Antonio's loud mouth and disrespect, and he's so afraid of her, he starts to clean up after himself.

Natalie has long talks with her sister at night on the patio. She learns about her brother-in-law's affairs, each one puncturing the happy home image she's always had of Rebecca's family. She tells her sister the man better leave town if he knows what's good for him. And she means it.

Val is still around, still a manager. Still an obnoxiously loud barfly, but I nudge her a bit to help Natalie get her old job back. It's practically the same crowd she started with, which is kind of unnerving, but nobody knows the mess she made in White Smoke. If anything, they think she can teach them a thing or two which makes Natalie giggle on the inside. She certainly can but not in the way they think.

She calls Hootie, trying to keep him involved in his kid's life even if it makes her stomach turn. But nobody returns her calls until the day Denise answers and tells her to leave them alone for good. She gets Natalie's address before slamming down the phone, and a week later, a check comes with Natalie's name on it. Ten grand. Hush money. Natalie opens a savings account, and puts it in the bank. She refers to it as "our future."

She calls Jerry. The first time his voice is sad, but the next few times it's lighter. He's been going to church regularly and meeting with a group of men Wednesday nights for Bible study. He's doing well at work and taking down the entire bowling community with his unstoppable strikes. He makes Natalie laugh, and there's a little seed planted there that continues to grow with every call. Jerry stops being just a "good guy" and moves into a different space in her heart. I give her time to realize what she has in somebody like him.

They decide to bury Rochelle. Wren actually decides and goes to Rochelle's old church to do it. She signs herself and Natalie up as members, and when word gets out that they're related to Ro, Ann snatches up their number and calls them immediately. They plan a proper burial in the church cemetery, and the whole church shows up for it. Natalie is shocked but in a really great way.

As with anything, there's always a time to reflect on the beginning. You can't live in the past. You can never ever change it, but you can hold it in your hands and peer into it. See where the colors started to fracture but always landing on where they blend as the world keeps spinning.

They plant their feet in the dirt, Natalie and Wren, on one particular day when the sky hovers between light and dark and curiosity gets the better of them. The air almost smells like it used to here when the three of them would sit on the front porch or Wren would grab the heart on his hand heading to the truck. But now they hold each other's hands, Wren's right one reaching for the tree hovering above her.

And she looks up.

Acknowledgements

First, credit where credit is due.

To Kitty Matz for not only offering to beta read but taking on the monumental task of proofreading this thing. I am so thankful for your generosity and friendship!

To my aunt, Danette Fortson, for not only reading and commenting on my book but for all of your prayers and open conversations on what it means to truly follow Christ.

To my beta readers: Aaron Cariño, Tara Androes Kelley, Whitney Harris, Matthew Miranda, and Holly Streck. I truly appreciate you all taking the time to read and for giving me your honest opinion of the book. You have no idea how your encouragement and kind words kept me going through this whole process!

To my parents, Mel and Maria Fortson, for always supporting me and sacrificing so I could hone the writing skills God gave me.

To my grandmother, Janet Paniagua, for constantly cheering me on.

To my best friend and sister from another mister, Meaghan Goldberg. You have such a big heart, and I'm so grateful to have you in my life.

To Matthew Clay, my husband who has to deal with the crazy side not everyone else gets to see. I love you and admire your extreme perseverance.

To Ava Clay, my daughter, who has seemed to have inherited a good portion of my genetic crazy. I'm so sorry, but Mommy still loves you.

Okay, so now for this part:

This was the hardest and easiest book I've written yet.

I know that's a loaded sentence.

It was hard because I had to revive it from the ashes. Scratch that. God revived it. I was all but through with writing. I just felt like I had

226

made a good go of it for ten plus years and that being a writer was no longer my calling. Maybe it never had been in the first place.

I had become a Christian at this point. I sure as heck wasn't going to write Christian romance novels. So what did I have any business being a writer anymore if everything I wrote had to be so sticky sweet?

God reminded me that not everything that's labeled Christian is about following Him. Maybe there was room in the market for characters who've seen their worst days and were about to see their best.

They just didn't know it yet.

So I had to dig through a lot of foul language (I used to be a sucker for the "f" word) and allow God to take the reins on this one. It was no longer about me writing the best thing since sliced bread just so my name would be the one seeking glory.

It became giving all the glory to Christ. Period. And for that reason, it was the easiest thing I've ever had to do.

We convolute this life. We want to ask a million questions when really there's only one we need to ask:

Are you for Him or are you against Him?

I want nothing but to be for Him. I want it more than I want to be a writer. I want it more than the breath in my lungs. Tomorrow will fall away but my love for Him won't.

Because I've finally realized, this isn't about me anymore.

Note: This is a fictional interpretation of what I believe Christ would observe in the situations presented in this book. I don't pretend to be Him or to receive any sort of special word from Him. I just opened my heart and asked Him what he needed me to write because I know the Holy Spirit had a book in store for me. I wholeheartedly believe everyone needs to read the Bible for themselves. Not a devotional. Not the regurgitated understanding of Scripture by someone who claims to be an authority figure. Read the Bible for YOURSELF. Do it. You will not regret it. And if you have any questions at all about following Jesus or feel you need to reach out for any reason, please contact me at authorericka@gmail.com. I will do my very best to get back to you in a timely manner.

My Testimony

I f you would have told me I would one day write a Christian fiction novel I would have laughed.

Hard.

I was raised Catholic and knew of God, but I eventually got to the point where I just didn't want to know Him anymore. I was fine being me, putting me first.

In fact, it was the only thing I lived for.

For those who aren't familiar, living like that eventually catches up to you. You can ignore it, push the dark feelings back into your mind's closet. But it's still there. An unsettling undercurrent that just never goes away.

My breaking point? Five years ago. We were living in Louisville and had managed to rack up $70,000 in debt. Mind you, we had previously been pretty flush and co-owned a growing business. But God allowed our missteps and greed to get the better of us, and soon we were looking at a whole mess of debt.

During this time I, of course, was writing the Great American Novel. It was going to be the best thing anyone had ever read, and therefore, was much more important than my friends, my family, and the niggling feeling that I should honor anything other than myself.

Ha. Fat chance.

I poured my entire soul into that book. I had landed an agent. It was sold to a small publishing house, a group of fellow writers I knew online who started their own literary imprint because every other "big time" publisher had turned down my glorious masterpiece.

Needless to say, the book wasn't a stellar success. It got published and even got some favorable reviews.

But it just seemed to...fizzle out.

So there I was: in debt, a literary failure, and nobody to blame but myself.

I turned to yoga to "chill out."

It became my religion, and it helped to numb the pain of the reality of my life, but there was still something missing.

Enter my sister-in-law.

She became extremely adamant that we go to church with her. Her church was a mega church, a ginormous building that I lovingly nicknamed "the monstrosity on the side of the road."

There was no way I was going to set foot in there.

Which I held true to...for a while.

Something strange started to happen. I started having demonic attacks.

I told you it was strange.

They happened at night when I was still awake. My body would become paralyzed, and I would will every cell in my body to move, but I couldn't. I couldn't speak. I couldn't scream. I could move my eyes only to glimpse my husband sound asleep as something that looked like a scaly gargoyle or alien being (I totally believe when people say they see aliens. I just don't think they are what they think they are) would slowly make its way toward me across the bedroom floor.

There was also the spinning.

I had been doing hardcore yoga up to this moment, and I think I nudged open some sort of "portal." I know that sounds like absolute lunacy (trust me), but I truly think I gave my heart to something other than God, and that particular thing found a way to weave its way in.

So sometimes, I'd be paralyzed and this feeling of buzzing energy would come over me, and the next thing I knew, it would feel like I was on top of the ceiling spinning around. My body was on the bed, I was aware of that, but *I* was not. That part was more frightening than seeing the demons because something about that power felt very wrong.

And yet, some part of me didn't want it to stop.

This went on for some time, and every evening, I'd say Jesus's name to make it go away. Yes, me. The girl who denied God and wanted nothing to do with Him. But oddly enough it all did go away whenever I said His name.

I just pretended it was a coincidence. You know, like any level-headed human who's being attacked in her own bedroom and spends her evenings spinning on her ceiling.

Or something.

I decided to go to my sister-in-law's church. I told myself it was just to placate her, but I knew it was something I needed on a very deep level. And the message I heard was an instant hit to the hurt: Jesus loved me.

Me.

A selfish thirty-year-old wannabe best selling writer who had absolutely no space in my life for Him.

Why?

It was the question I continued to chew on as the days wore on and the demons continued their onslaught. I convinced my husband that we needed to keep going on Sundays, something he was reluctant to agree to at first, but eventually decided it couldn't hurt. What else were we doing on Sundays?

A change began to occur in me. My heart softened. The old bravado of who I was and everything that defined me began to melt away.

Finally, for the first time, it was just me and God. And there's not much posturing you can do when you realize the immensity of something like that.

So one night, three months in, I gave my life to Christ. I was in my bed, covers to my chin, deeply terrified of the night ahead. But I knew innately that I didn't have to keep shouldering this burden. So I gave it all to Him.

That night? I slept soundly for the first time in a long time, and I haven't seen the demons since.

One of my biggest roadblocks to ever considering following Jesus was the corny, sugar-coated American Christian lifestyle one seems to adopt when making this decision. Rest assured, that facade is a total lie. My life has been nothing but a deep commitment to Jesus and the gritty endurance it takes to sacrifice for others.

There is nothing sugary sweet about denying yourself for the glory of God.

But what does exist is the covering of His love and protection and the promises He affords us. At the time I gave myself to Christ, we had gone from being on top of the world financially to living in debt. I knew that as soon as I submitted to Christ, He was going to open doors for us to get back in good standing.

Today? We're out of debt completely and set to pay off our house in the next three years.

No magic wand. No prosperity gospel. Just a good Father that's equipped us every move we've made in His name.

I could go on and tell you all the unbelievable things that have happened since that night when I was terrified and gave it all to Christ. But then we'd be here for days. Instead, I leave you with a prayer. That you will search your own heart, give up your own pretenses and the idea of what you have to be in this life. This world is nothing if not a liar and will do anything to keep its claws in you. Release them through confession and following Jesus alone.

Because weeping may come in the night, but joy comes in the morning.

Proceeds & Reviews

Ten percent of the proceeds for this book will go directly to The Call in Northwest Arkansas, an organization that seeks to equip, educate and encourage the Christian community to provide a future and a hope to His children in state foster care in Arkansas. Please consider giving *A Violent Hope* a review wherever the book was purchased to help spread the word!

Don't miss out!

Visit the website below and you can sign up to receive emails whenever Ericka Clay publishes a new book. There's no charge and no obligation.

https://books2read.com/r/B-A-YUDL-OSKIB

BOOKS 2 READ

Connecting independent readers to independent writers.

About the Author

Ericka Clay is a published novelist and the author of *Unkept* and *Dear Hearts*. She has been awarded a number of times by Writers Digest for various short fiction pieces and placed as a quarter-finalist in the 2010 Amazon Breakthrough Novel Award contest for her novel, *Cooper Cooper*.

Ericka lives in Northwest Arkansas with her husband, daughter, two dogs and an insatiable need to push buttons, both figuratively and literally. You can find Ericka at @erickaclaywrites on Facebook and Instagram.

Also, do you love podcasts? Ericka has just launched her Ask the Author podcast on all major podcasting platforms, including iTunes!

Read more at erickaclay.com.

About the Publisher

Believable Books is a publishing imprint that seeks to fill a very noticeable gap in the Christian publishing industry: raw, real stories with a redemptive element.

In short: we won't be publishing Amish romances any time soon.

We will, however, be publishing contemporary fiction that follows gritty characters from their rock bottoms all the way to their God-glorifying tops.

Believable Books seeks to bring light to a dark literary world, with grace, hope and the redemptive love of Christ always at at the core.

You can find Believable Books on Twitter at @believablebooks.